Advance Praise for
The Phoenix and the Firebird

"With cinematographic crispness, this romantic vision of a distant time and culture conjures up a tale of friendship, family, and magic. Stay up all night to read it, and you'll freshly understand the old Russian adage, 'The morning is wiser than the night.' I was enchanted."

— Gregory Maguire, author of *Wicked*

"A joy from start to finish! The world was brilliantly imagined, the plot filled with excitement (stick oracles, riddles, corpse-walkers, rope ladders, forest spirits) and I loved the fusion of Chinese and Russian folklore. A vivid and exciting adventure story — kids will love it!"

— Abi Elphinstone, author of *Sky Song*

"A Peking caught between an imperial city and a new republic; a world where harsh reality mingles with myth and magic. Warlords, exiled Russians, gangsters, a child in search of her father. There are worlds within worlds in old Peking — real and imagined. Kossiakoff and Crawford bring them all together and to life."

— Paul French, author of *Midnight in Peking and City of Devils*

"Russian sojourner Lucy in chaotic warlord-ruling China embarks on a perilous feat to rescue her father from a warlord's clutches, with the help of her witty Chinese friend Su. Mythical friends and foes appear to aid and thwart their attempt. One can't but root for the two undeterred friends. The magical story, told in melodic prose, held this reader rapt with wonder throughout! An absolute gem of a read!"
— Alice Poon, author of *The Heavenly Sword* and *The Earthly Blaze*

"*The Phoenix and the Firebird* is an exquisitely written, deliciously fun, and often moving historical fantasy novel that follows Lucy, a brave young refugee of the Russian Civil War, on her quest to find and free her captive father. The story transports us to an early 20th century China of myth and magic: Along her journey from Beijing into an eerie forest and beyond, Lucy will encounter a fascinating, terrifying, eye-popping array of figures from traditional Russian and Chinese folklore, all of whom are brought beautifully and viscerally to life by co-authors Alexis Kossiakoff and Scott Forbes Crawford.

Readers with any familiarity with Russian and Chinese fairy tales will find so much to delight in here; readers without, so much to discover. Richly steeped in these mythologies, The Phoenix and the Firebird is a gripping, touching story about sacrifice, bravery, belief, and the meaning of home, that will enchant and mesmerize readers from middle-grade to adulthood. Highly, highly recommended."
— Kristen Loesch, author of *The Last Russian Doll*

"Crawford and Kossiakoff guide us on a magical journey through Chinese and Russian folklore that is welcoming to readers of all ages. It's like an epic film that has come alive on the page."
— Susan Blumberg-Kason, author of *Bernardine's Shanghai Salon*

"Immersive and captivating, the hidden treasures within the pages of this multi-faceted historical fantasy will enchant readers of all ages. The seamless weaving together of Chinese and Russian folk-tales makes for a lush tapestry of mythic resonance; foregrounded by an immensely human tale of the search for lost family, and the finding of friends in unexpected places. Lucy and Su are likeable, relatable heroines, and the backdrop of 1920s China is as evocative and enchanting as the mythic figures that help and hinder the two friends on their journey."

— Viki Holmes, author of *Girls' Adventure Stories of Long Ago*

"Beautifully written and meticulously researched, *The Phoenix and the Firebird* — inspired by the authors' own family histories and experiences — is a gripping and emotional read, following the story of Lucy, a Russian refugee in 1920s Beijing who is waiting for her father to join her so they can build a new life together. But when he's taken prisoner by a ferocious warlord, Lucy must set out on a dangerous journey to try to find out what has happened to him, her only clue a scarlet feather said to belong to a creature from a fairy tale — the legendary firebird…

With its richly realised settings, action-packed plot, and cleverly integrated elements of Russian and Chinese folklore and philosophy, this novel is sure to appeal enormously to young readers — and to older readers too! Although the setting is a historical one, the themes of displacement, and of courage in the face of adversity, give the novel a fresh and current feel. And Lucy is a protagonist a modern audience will instantly relate to and find themselves cheering on as she goes in search of her beloved father, undergoes a series of challenges, and, somewhere along the way, discovers the strength within herself."

— Emma Pass, author and editor

THE PHOENIX AND THE FIREBIRD

Alexis Kossiakoff
Scott Forbes Crawford

EARNSHAW
BOOKS

The Phoenix and the Firebird

By Alexis Kossiakoff and Scott Forbes Crawford

ISBN-13: 978-988-8843-38-1

FICTION

Cover design © 2024 by Dinara Mirtalipova

EB205

Published in Hong Kong by Earnshaw Books Ltd.

*To Alexander Kossiakoff, whose childhood journey
inspired the authors of this book.*

*And to our Vivian, whose journey continues to
inspire her parents.*

PROLOGUE

October 17, 1920

To my little squirrel,

I am writing from the city of Harbin, on the northern tip of one of China's stretched fingers. I have traveled a very long way to get here. By train, by horse, and on my feet, and my journey is far from over. Not until I see you will it be complete. I will swim across rivers, I will chase leopards and sneak past sleeping tigers. I will even track the Firebird through the forest if I must. After the three years we have been apart, nothing will stop me from joining you.

The civil war in Russia has cost us so much, and we have lost to the Bolsheviks. No cause is worth so many mothers' tears, so I have left the army and ordered my soldiers to escape if they can. There is no way our family could survive under the new rulers, so I have no regrets about sending you away to safety in China. Except for the trial of being separated from you.

I will leave Harbin Thursday and arrive at the Peking train station on Saturday at 3:30 p.m.

While my heart feels empty to abandon our cherished land, it is no longer the place we loved. Our home is gone. But somewhere, I believe we shall find a new one.

With unbounded excitement and all my love,

Papa

1

THE TEMPLE

It didn't start with the letter. Not exactly. The whole business with the warlord, the fox whose number of tails Su and I even today disagree about, and escaping the gigantic birdcage — all of that came to pass after I found the feather. But maybe I should come to that a little later, because that day when the mailman delivered Papa's letter, I would have laughed at the very idea of magic.

I savored Papa's handwriting, which hadn't changed a bit, with the swirling strokes of his fountain pen reminding me of waltzing dancers spilling their champagne. Then I dashed off to tell Su, weaving among the tall pots of fermenting soybeans and winter cabbages dotting the stone courtyard between our houses and knocking on her door. No answer. I peered through a hole in the rice-paper window, sweeping across the tables crammed with Chinese calligraphy and the snaking piles of ancient books crowding the floor.

There was no sign of Su. I'd have to check our hideout.

Our houses stood on a *hutong*, one of the hundreds of narrow alleyways unique to Peking. They are like a giant outdoor living room, shared by all the people of the city. Making my way down the street, I passed a storyteller entertaining a circle of kids, next to a man selling tea from a canister he wore like a backpack. I turned the corner to find people of all ages gossiping as they sat on stools bundled up against the wind, and the neighborhood cobbler fixing a woman's shoe while she balanced on a single leg like a heron. "Lucy, where are you off to in such a hurry?" he called to me.

"Looking for Su, Mr Wen."

"Haven't seen her. You know, your Chinese is getting much better!"

"Thanks," I smiled, "I've got to go, there's big news!"

I stopped at the withered old poplar, scanning in all directions. Seeing no one nearby, I scrambled up the tree and warily stepped onto the tiled roof of a house, then hoisted myself onto the crumbling wall of our temple. I inched along the ledge, the only way in since the gate was sealed, just like the day a year ago when Su Feng — that was her full name, but I always just called her Su — and I had discovered this place. There were many abandoned shrines, temples and imperial buildings sprinkled around Peking, forgotten ever since the Chinese emperor fell from power eight years ago. Ours had a slanted roof and two small chambers that opened onto a stone-floored garden with weeds wrestling their way to the daylight, and a pond of greenish water. It was dusty, full of shadows and spooky at night — not an obvious hideout for two girls.

As I stood over the temple garden, I saw Su sitting below, brushing Chinese characters on a sheet of paper, her forearms flexing with each stroke. All her movements seemed deliberate, focused and fluid, graceful yet firm. Sweat gleamed on her forehead and her two waist-length braids were tousled, evidence of the martial-arts routine she must have just completed, if the long staff and wooden sword resting beside her weren't giveaways.

I always hated the next part, placing my rear on the top of the wall and then leaping off. I spilled when I hit the ground, my hands flailing to break my fall. No sooner had I landed and dusted my palms on my dress than Su set aside her brush. "Hi, Lucy. Oh, what's happened?"

That's a true friend – knowing what you're feeling before you do. Taking the letter from my pocket I translated it the best I could from Russian into Chinese. "After all this time, your father is coming today! How wonderful!" Su's brow knit. "So why do you look like someone just kicked you in the stomach?"

I hadn't realized that I appeared anything other than excited. But there was no use trying to hide anything from Su, it would be like trying to trick a fox. "I'm so happy, Su, I feel like if I don't hold on to something I'll start floating away. But I'm also... nervous, I guess. I mean, look at my shoes – they've got holes in them." I tugged on my dark chin-length bob. "And last time Papa saw me, I had a long ponytail."

"Ah, you are afraid he won't recognize you, is that it? I've never met the man but I am sure he's changed, too. Anyway, he'd have to be half-blind not to know you. I can't imagine there will be too many big-nose girls running around the train station."

I pretended to protest at her teasing me by using the slang for foreigner – 'big-nose'. But a little laughter was what I needed. "The train comes in at three-thirty and it's barely noon now. I don't know how I'm supposed to wait."

"You've waited three years, Lucy!"

"It's different somehow."

"Hey, I know what this moment calls for." She got that smirk of hers. "Something that smells like an old man's shoe."

My mouth watered. "You'd do that for me? Really?"

"This one time. But you'll owe me. I don't even like being near the stuff."

She was talking about *ch'ou toufu* – which translates to 'stinky bean curd' – a Chinese delicacy. Let's say it's an acquired taste,

3

and even Su turns up her nose. But I don't know what's wrong with her, because to me it's heavenly. And embracing such parts of Peking life gave me a feeling I truly belonged here, that I wasn't merely some homeless girl blown to China by a cruel wind. Anyhow, stinky bean curd was just the recipe for getting me through the next few hours.

"I don't have to work until four o'clock," she went on. "We can find somewhere near the train station that's also on the way for me." Su washed dishes at a fancy restaurant catering to foreigners and rich Chinese. For generations, her family had served in the imperial court. When the empire fell, so did Su's family fortunes and position in society. Overnight they went from being government ministers and military commanders to garbage carriers, shoeshines and beggars. Once her father had been an imperial librarian, but he'd since grown sick with consumption ravaging his lungs. And like mine, Su's mother had died long ago. So it fell on Su to earn money and take care of him. I suspect she felt a bond with me because she, too, understood what it felt like to lose everything. At least I could continue at school. Su wasn't as lucky, though her father personally instructed her in the great literature of China and every day critiqued her calligraphy like she had just finished practicing today.

I watched her tidy up, swirling her writing brushes in a bowl, squeezing the water from the bristles, then placing the brushes in the sun to dry. As she rolled up her calligraphy and put away her practice weapons in one of the chambers, I realized how lucky we were to have found this place. Here in the temple, we were not one big-nose and one Chinese, we were simply two kids, with no rules we had to follow and no expectations from our countrymen about whom it was proper to be friends with.

Su helped lift me onto the roof and we scurried along the wall. Peking is low slung, with very few houses reaching above a single story. Though the Drum Tower now rose to our left, looming above the neighborhood, pounding the hour for the city dwellers, so they would know when to go off to work or when they could catch a performance at one of the city's opera houses. I'd heard talk of the drums being replaced by a Western-style clock, even though the Tower had been giving the time for centuries. But I, of all people, know how things that seem permanent can come to a sudden end.

We dropped from the wall to the street. Peking born and bred, Su knew every shortcut and led the way. We slalomed past donkey-carts and bicycles, cars and rickshaws (they're a kind of carriage pulled by a man instead of a horse) and strolled through an outdoor barbershop. Passing an abandoned house, I noticed on its side a figure painted in black, a sort of monstrous, four-legged beast with two horns sprouting out its head. It made me shiver and I noticed Su darken and turn away.

We slipped through an alley so narrow I could touch both walls. "So, after all this time," said Su, "what are you looking forward to most about seeing your father?"

"I want him to tell me stories. My father was the best storyteller in the city. You'd never believe a colonel in the army, who's been in all kinds of battles, could also spin a story like he does! He'd make a man whose house is on fire stop to hear his tale before running to safety."

"What kind of stories?"

Pushing into a crowd, I trailed her. Maneuvering past vendors selling candied crabapples on long sharp sticks, steamed buns and savory pancakes. Hawkers shouted their wares and services, the knife-sharpeners, tailors, and fruit salesmen, each making the peculiar singsong call of their trade.

"Russian fairytales, mostly," I said, raising my voice over the din. "He'd sit at the edge of my bed before I went to sleep, telling me about the adventures of Vasilisa the Beautiful, the dreadful witch Baba Yaga, and the Frog Princess. And of course, the Firebird. A magical creature with mysterious powers that many brave heroes tried to capture. He even mentioned it in his letter, because that story is my favorite of them all."

What I didn't share with Su, as we marched into the heart of the city, was that every night before I drifted off to sleep, I would tell myself Papa's stories. Somehow, I'd believed keeping the tales alive would keep him safe, too, as though the words could be forged into thick armor.

I should have known better.

2

THE ENCOUNTER

Its proper name in Chinese means "Gate of the Pure Sun" but most people call the massive structure *Ch'ienmen* ("Front Gate"), and I prefer that because once it was the doorway between two worlds. Gray and indomitable, four stories tall, it had four rows of thirteen windows stretching across its width, like dozens of eyes scanning for any approaching trouble. As the guardhouse to the Forbidden City palace where Chinese emperors had ruled, only people on official business would dare cross its threshold. Today, though, with the emperors long gone, Su and I walked through its tunnel-like passage and threw ourselves into the chaos of Dashilar beyond.

The Dashilar neighborhood immediately felt different from the straight, orderly Peking streets I was familiar with. Here, the streets curved and zigzagged crazily like untamed rivers, with alleyways darting in and out like snapping eels. Ancient and modern smashed together, with cars and trucks honking as they tried to wrest the road away from the long caravans of camels chained nose to nose, accompanied by merchants wrapped in sheepskins and furry hats, who looked like they had just wandered off a Mongolian plain. Each camel hauled a huge load of cargo stuffed between their two humps. Wheat, wool, sacks of coal, and fat casks of rice wine peeked out between the bulging packs.

Passing one of the camels idly chewing while its driver haggled with a customer, I scrunched my nose and turned to Su. "Look, there's foamy dribble coming out of his mouth."

Her eyes bulged. "That's not all, Lucy — watch out, he's going to spit!" I leaped away just before the camel honked like a car and spat a cannonball of yellow-green saliva.

"Su, you could have warned me!"

"I *did!*"

"I mean, that those creatures could spit farther than a sailor."

"Everyone knows camel do that." She shrugged. "Or maybe not everyone. Come on, this way."

Cutting through the bustle, I heard mingled song and rowdy cheering as we neared an opera house. It was painted in rich golds and reds, and outside it the parked vehicles ranged from rickshaws to a fancy motorcar gleaming in the sun like a black mirror. A side door giving a view of the stage stood open and we stopped to watch. All manner of people made up the audience. Rich men with slicked-backed hair and fancy Western suits cheered the performers alongside sweaty rickshaw-pullers and everyone in between, united in their love of Peking opera.

Musicians sat on the stage blowing into their flutes, strumming stringed instruments and clanging bells and gongs. The actors, each in elaborate costumes, and some wearing rods attached to their backs that resembled insects' antennae, pulled off acrobatic tricks, dueled with swords and told jokes. Each one of the actors wore a vibrant mask of face paint, which combined many colors, but mostly red, white, green, and black. I couldn't take my eyes off the performance, until an usher appeared inside, spotted us enjoying the free show, and grinning, wagged a finger at us before shutting the door.

We turned a corner and I looked across the intersection into a long alley. Just as once the Ch'ienmen Gate was a barrier between the imperial realm and the world everyone else had to live in, this intersection sat right on top of an invisible but firm line I knew never to cross. Down that road lurked the Badlands. The most treacherous neighborhood in Peking. A shore on which all sorts of broken human driftwood washed up. A place where darkness feasts on misery — on a good day. The street was empty. Probably because the night creatures of the Badlands hadn't woken up yet.

Then, walking along, something caught my eye and chilled me to the bone.

There it was again, painted on a brick wall. The same symbol I'd seen before. That horned monster was following me like a sinister shadow. I was thinking of asking Su about it but something told me she still didn't want to talk about it. "So, how will we find a place for stinky bean curd?" I asked instead.

"The nose never lies."

She was right. The pungent, almost rotting, but oddly appealing smell wafted to me. Soon we came to a tiny shack with tables and benches set out on the street, where diners feasted on bean curd and other snacks. We squeezed onto one of the long wooden benches, joining five other diners who looked up, regarded us a moment, and then returned to munching and slurping their snacks.

The owner, a woman clad in an exquisite traditional Chinese coat, sauntered over. With her regal, almost stuffy air, she didn't seem to fit here. "What would you like?" she asked Su, giving me a suspicious side glance.

"A big bowl of fried stinky bean curd, please," I said.

Turning to me she instantly warmed up. "Oh, you speak Chinese! Most foreigners here just bark like dogs in their own languages, expecting us to understand."

Still curious, I asked if this stand had always been hers. She smiled sadly. "Once, it was not this place I owned, but a grand mansion. I made trips to the Forbidden City to see my cousins there."

"You were royalty?" I exclaimed.

"In another age," the lady said wistfully. She then noticed my patched dress that I'd outgrown months ago. "There's a saying in Chinese: 'Those who survive hard times will later meet good fortune.' I suppose it is something we must all remember." With a small smile she went away and soon returned with my order.

"I can't believe you actually like eating that," said Su, shaking her head as I was about to take a bite.

But I never did get a chance to enjoy my bean curd.

Suddenly everyone in the restaurant looked just like cats chased by stray dogs. Two burly scoundrels swaggered in, one Chinese with a scowl so deep it would need a chisel to undo, the other European whose hard piggy eyes showed the true unfriendly nature of his wide smile. Both wore clothes similar to military uniforms, and their jackets showed a small, embroidered black emblem.

It was the very same monster design I'd seen painted on the walls.

The owner swallowed and held up her hands pleadingly. "Please, I don't have enough. Isn't next week acceptable?"

Cackling, Piggy Eyes said in broken Chinese, "Ha, she thinks we are *asking* for the money." He then spat a nasty word in Russian that made my blood boil — the mannerless brute was from my part of the world.

"You see this?" The Chinese goon tapped the emblem on his jacket. "Remember it. Soon everything in this city will belong to The Taotie."

I heard Su grind her jaw. "You stay where you are, Lucy," she whispered. Sensing what she was about to do I tried to grab her, but I was too late. She stood, glaring at the goons. "Why don't you two go away? You stink even worse than this bean curd." Her voice was firm, but I could hear the slightest quaver in it.

Everyone there, the diners and goons alike, froze as if Su had just cast a spell. I thought maybe through her iron nerve she had put an end to this nasty scene. But then the Russian reached into his back pocket—and when his hand came back something flashed in it.

It was a knife!

The sight of that ugly blade, and the even uglier grin on his face, turned my legs to wood. But not Su's. She only stared harder at him, like her eyes were sharper and more dangerous than his puny weapon. And maybe because she barely reacted to this threat, her confidence spread, for in the next moment a bench squeaked as a stocky bricklayer got to his feet. Then another man stood, then a woman, then another person, and another, again and again.

Now facing not one girl but a crowd of ten, the goons muttered to each other and Piggy Eyes slowly put away his knife. "Let's see how brave you are when we own the city," he said, "because the Taotie is coming."

Even after the two men strode off, it took everyone in the stand a few moments to sit again. The owner came over and thanked Su profusely. I was still too stunned to speak, and I staggered off with Su guiding me by the wrist. "You're crazy, but that was amazing!" I gushed to Su, at last getting my words back.

But she was in no mood to celebrate. "People like those two make me sick. My country has become like a shattered vase, with gangsters and bandits scrambling for the biggest piece, tormenting the Chinese people along the way. I don't know what can be done to stop it." Su hung her head, something I'd never seen before.

"And who's this 'Taotie' they were talking about?" I asked. It wasn't a pair of sounds I'd come across before in Chinese.

"No, Lucy, it's pronounced 'tao-tee-yeh.' The Taotie is a Chinese creature from mythology, representing greed. Their designs are on some ancient bronze cauldrons. Now there's a warlord who's named himself after that."

"Warlord?"

"A sort of bandit king," she answered. "I've heard rumors of this Taotie before. He's been taking over the countryside. And he makes the men out there serve in his private army, whether they wish to or not. He's been pushing towards the city. The fact those two men of his were here must mean he's getting closer."

"I'm ashamed one of them was Russian. I can't imagine what my father would say about that."

Su brightened a little. "Speaking of your father, you'd better hurry. Let's forget about what just happened, you are about to be so joyful! And I must get to work. But I'll see you tonight?" I was so relieved when she added, "I wonder if his nose is even bigger than yours?"

I rolled my eyes at the joke. "Come to my house tonight and find out for yourself."

3

THE FEATHER

The big clock over the train station read 3:25 p.m. —I was just in time. Compared to the ancient Chinese buildings nearby, the modern station, with a tower like part of a storybook castle off on one side, didn't really look like it belonged in Peking. A bit like me.

I heaved open the heavy doors. Inside, travelers and their luggage jammed the waiting hall, the dim electric lighting making it resemble a strangely crowded cave deep in the Earth. Clutter carpeted the waiting room floor: sunflower seed shells, yesterday's newspapers, and dumped tea leaves that had been steeped too many times and perfumed the air with a bitter pungency.

In the far corner of the waiting room stood a tall European man, his broad back to me. He wore a dapper gray suit and a wide-brimmed, dark blue hat. Could it be Papa? But it wasn't time yet. Maybe the train had arrived early!

I ran over, grinning ear to ear, and was just about to throw my arms around him when the figure turned. I gasped, halting. A long shiny scar ran down his face like a bolt of frozen lightning. A pair of icy blue eyes stared at me —or rather *into* me, for I felt like he was judging and weighing my soul. I'd never seen him before but that face could only belong to one man —Vlad the Deathless. Every Russian in Peking heard whispers about their scarred, fierce-eyed countryman who ruled half the city's criminal underworld. Vlad was called "The Deathless" because the many attempts on his life all had failed. The gangster raised an eyebrow with an amused look as I stumbled backwards. Mumbling "Sorry" in Russian, I hurried away.

Positioning myself on a bench in the waiting room, I fidgeted, unable to sit still. I was still feeling unsettled after my encounter with Vlad. Though he was now across the station, I felt his eyes following me. My worries deepened as the train grew later and later — 3:40, 3:55, 4:30 all crawled past. But then at last the thin cry of a train whistle brought me jumping to my feet. I rushed onto the platform just as the locomotive wheezed into the station and screeched to a stop, groaning and hissing steam like some wounded iron dragon. The side of the train was all dinged up, holes and gouges scattered about, and some windows had spider-web patterns of cracks, while others were smashed outright.

Something was wrong. I felt like it was not really me standing there, but someone in a play or a book, because whatever terrible thing I was about to experience, surely *I* didn't deserve it.

The train doors opened.

No one came out. At first.

Then a few older people, women and small children trickled from the train. A nameless dread filled me as I saw their hollow eyes.

Back in Russia I'd seen that look before. And hoped to never see it again.

I tried to ask a few other people what was happening, but they were too distressed to answer. Then Vlad stormed up to a disheveled train conductor and gripped him by the shirt. The conductor murmured something, to which I heard the gangster growl in flawless Chinese, "I don't care what happened to the men, who stole my horse?!"

Through quaking lips the conductor gasped a name that would have meant nothing to me the day before.

The Taotie.

The warlord who was trying to capture Peking. The one whose goons Su had stood up to at the restaurant.

Instantly Vlad's knotted hands fell from the poor man, who scurried off. The gangster was in such a state of shock he didn't notice me at his side. I summoned up some courage, and I tugged his arm. "What is happening?"

His penetrating eyes lanced into mine. "The train was attacked by the warlord known as Taotie. He has kidnapped all the men aboard to serve in his army."

My heart and lungs clumped together, smothering me. "But my father was on the train!"

"I presume your father was a man, then?" he said cuttingly. "Thus, he is now in the warlord's army. It is said the Taotie prefers Russian soldiers fighting for him. At least he has good sense in that."

"But how... ?"

He cut me off. "Look, young one, perhaps Fate smiled on your father and he missed the train. Perhaps not. Either way, it is not my affair, and my own demands attention. Someone will give me answers." He stormed off.

A half hour passed before two policemen appeared, and my heart soared—until they heard "Taotie" from a woman sobbing for her missing husband, and almost immediately drifted away. Clearly, they wanted nothing to do with this. So I had to see for myself.

I climbed aboard the train, wading through the swamp of clothing, luggage, foods, and books strewn everywhere. Moving from car to car, I scanned every seat, not knowing what I was seeking except for some sign of Papa. But there was nothing. At least until I came to the last car, and I saw it on a seat, as if it had just fluttered down from the sky moments before. In that moment, I knew Papa had indeed been on this train—and that he needed my help.

It was a single scarlet-gold feather. Papa had described the magical Firebird many times when telling me Russian fairy tales. Somehow, he must have had this made for me. A gift. I knew such a creature could bring doom or good fortune depending on its mood, but finding a Firebird feather only meant one thing: the beginning of a quest.

I stuffed it inside my pocket and hurried out to search for my father.

4

THE DOLL

My clothes were clammy with sweat as I wound through the alleys leading to my house. I could barely breathe once I reached my door.

The house was nothing like the grand St. Petersburg apartment I had lived in before fleeing to China. In my old home, I had to throw open the heavy velvet drapes and look out on the snow to know it was winter, for servants made our home toasty by keeping the stove and the *samovar*, a traditional water heater for tea, piping hot. Here, some panes in the window missing their glass had been papered over, barely keeping out the howling gusts of wind.

A lamp burned inside and the round silhouette of Madam Korchigina waddled past the window. A governess in St. Petersburg, the "affectionate" lady offered to take charge of me until I was reunited with Papa. He hired her—and after I said goodbye to him, she immediately gave up her kind act. As the train steamed from Russia to China, she barked at me, making clear she would tolerate me, and no more than that. If I became troublesome, I could find somewhere else to live—despite the fact that the money Papa provided for my living expenses covered the rent of this house.

She was seated in her plush chair, sipping tea. As I entered, she released one of her infamous annoyed sighs. "Where have you been? I hope not running around with that *local* girl again. Such things would never be permitted in the old country."

Usually when she called Su a "local" I lashed out—it had a nasty ring, as if the people who were actually from China somehow didn't belong here. But I just stood there. I was too defeated even to speak.

"What's wrong with you?" asked Korchigina, almost feigning concern. I tried to speak but only managed to gulp air, and I fished the letter from my pocket. "Well, where is he? Did anyone tell you anything?" she asked after reading it.

"The train was robbed." My voice began to crack, and when I saw relief wash over her cabbage-like face, I ran into the bedroom. She was the last person I wanted to see me cry.

I felt as cold and gloomy as the house itself. Keeping my coat on, for the room was barely warmer than outside, I plunked onto my sleeping pallet, trying not to let myself think of the soft bed with down coverlet that in St Petersburg had so easily carried me off to sleep. Though an hour went by, I couldn't nod off, my head was a whirlpool of thoughts, sucking me further into despair. Papa used to always say that living life is not like crossing a meadow. I was lucky to have survived the war, and Papa was right, life would never be easy, but there were certain days when the walls felt like hands around my neck. And tonight they had no mercy, they were strangling me. I needed to get out.

Through a crack in the door I peered out on Madam Korchigina. She was dozing in a chair. I blew out the candle, grabbed some clothes and arranged them into a mound on my pallet, then covered it with a blanket. That ought to fool her into thinking I was there sleeping. Then opening the window, I slipped out into the crisp, dark air. The night sky was a pageant of darkness and light, clouds gathering in huge numbers, the moon struggling to sneak a few of its beams past them.

I picked up three stones from the ground and placed them on Su's windowsill, then tapped the frame so Su would come and notice. One stone signaled that she should come to my house, two stones meant to meet at the temple, and three to meet at the temple for an emergency meeting. I ran down the lane and climbed the poplar tree, just like a *belushka*, the "little squirrel"Papa liked to call me, I thought bitterly. Jumping from rooftop to rooftop, I came to the old temple and dropped in.

Inside the temple, I pried up a loose stone of the floor. In the small hollow below I kept one of the few treasures I'd taken from Russia. My doll, Luba. I removed her from her cotton pouch. She wasn't much to look at now, scuffed and coated with grime as if she'd stumbled out of some desert. Once, she'd been a beauty. Especially on that sunny spring morning four years ago when we'd first met. What a welcome surprise to find her in my bed beside me. In that moment she almost helped me forget the first thought I'd had every morning for months: *How is Mama today?* Illness had been eating away at my mother, each day leaving her paler than the last.

Before going to check on Mama, I took some time to study my new friend. She had golden locks and rosy cheeks and red, heart-shaped lips punctuated her porcelain skin. Her eyes resembled a cloudless sky between the long black lashes. She wore an ankle-length white lace dress with pink silk roses sewn to the bodice and a matching silk sash. "Luba, that's what I'll call you," I'd whispered, giving her the name, "My Dear." I was cuddling her when the floorboards in the hallway squeaked outside my door. Slow footsteps approached, then paused outside my room for a minute or more before the door opened. "Good morning, Papa," I had said. "Was this doll a gift from you? I — "

His face was like a pit of ashes. Even before he spoke, I knew the truth and clutched Luba to me.

One week after my mother's funeral, I asked my father again about the doll. But he had no idea where she had come from. "Your mother must have decided to give you one last gift," he guessed. "Though I don't know how she found the strength to come to your room, let alone go out and buy this doll."

Sitting now on the stone floor of the temple, I hugged Luba tight. Even though I had long outgrown playing with her, she was still precious to me. Not only because she reminded me of my mother, but because of what was hidden inside her. When I left St Petersburg, there was not much of my old life I could take with me. Papa had sent a telegram from the Siberian front, telling my nanny to prepare me to board a train to China the next day because it was no longer safe. After the nanny had gone to sleep, I crept to my father's room and found my mother's old jewelry box in the back of the dresser drawer. I grabbed a handful of the finest pieces and ran back to my room. I had heard of women hiding jewels by sewing them in the hems of their skirts. Such a trick would be too obvious with the thin material of a young girl's dress. My eyes roamed the bedroom until settling upon my treasured doll. I figured even the Red soldiers would not be cruel enough to take a little girl's toy. It was risky, and I hated the thought of having to damage Luba, but I knew it was the only way to protect the jewels. I grabbed a maid's sewing basket and took out sharp scissors, carefully making an incision into the doll's back, removed some stuffing and replaced it with the jewels. With a surgeon's precision I sewed Luba back up again, leaving her much heavier, and only faintly scarred. Someday, the jewels inside her would buy Papa and me a new life somewhere. My doll was a link to my old life – to Russia, and to my mother. And she was also my ticket to a new life.

Now as I held Luba in my lap, her heaviness weighed upon me like a stone, and I found, of course, that she was little help in this situation. I had to do whatever I could to find Papa. Waiting was not an option and holding onto an old toy wouldn't help. I placed her back in her hiding spot and tried to think of what I must do next. No ideas came, but luckily, I soon heard feet pattering across the roof. Su jumped down and sat down beside me, her eyes wide with surprise. "I saw the stones. What are you doing here? Why aren't you with your father?"

I told her the whole story: the empty train, meeting the gangster Vlad, even about the feather. She asked to see it, examining the feather closely, as if there might be some secret message scrawled on the quill, but then just shook her head. "It's a phoenix feather, that much is clear."

"What do you mean? It's a Firebird feather! Aren't they the same thing anyway?"

Su gasped, placing her hand on her collarbone in feigned disbelief. "Did I just hear those words, Lucy? Is your Chinese failing you? Did you dare compare your apple-thieving Firebird to the *fenghuang*, the regal phoenix? A creature of the upmost virtue and grace?"

I sighed. "Are we really arguing about this right now?" I love Su, but sometimes her timing could drive me crazy. Maybe she was trying to get me to think of something else, to give me a moment of comfort from the turmoil and terror convulsing me.

Su gave a sly smile. "We will see who's right, just be patient." I shrugged, and nodded, not in the mood for bickering. She then looked directly at me and her smile sank away. "This situation is not good, Lucy, not good at all. I've been asking around about this Taotie character and he is serious trouble."

"You don't need to tell me that—he kidnapped my father!" I'd hoped Su would offer me some consoling words or even have a solution to my problem. Instead, as she went on, I felt only more desolate.

"That wicked warlord has set his greedy eyes on Peking, and I don't think there is much that can be done to stop him. He is raising the fiercest army imaginable. Whether his soldiers are willing, or like your father, they're not." She paused for a moment, then leaned in as if telling a secret. "And the Taotie is beyond evil. He is not just a regular outlaw or warlord. They say he has 'powers.'"

"What do you mean?"

"He can harness the spirit world. Something like that. He lives in a hidden fortress where he keeps his army. He is very superstitious and is famous for wearing three dried monkey heads around his waist as protection."

I cringed. "Does that work?"

Su shrugged. "Well, it seems to have so far."

"But I can't sit around and do nothing, Su. My father is being held prisoner by an evil man wearing shriveled monkey heads."

"I know." Su stared into the night sky, growing very still.

"There must be something we can do," I said softly.

She drew a long breath and seemed to come to a decision of some sort. "Okay. If you really have no leads to go on, there might be someone who can help us. *Might*—I can't make any promises. But you'll have to be prepared to see things a little differently."

5

THE PROPHECY

The brilliant colors, loud noises and hubbub of the temple nearly overwhelmed my senses. People thronged the entrance. We waded into that vast river of humanity and instantly, were swept along by its current through the gate. Su swam in like an expert, while I struggled like a puppy paddling to keep up.

It was a kaleidoscope of activity inside. Half of Peking seemed to be stuffed into the temple grounds, from newborn babies to ancient couples who, judging by their lined faces, must have been more than a century old. Here vendors offered a bewildering variety of goods: hand-carved wooden toys, traditional Chinese paintings, porcelain pots with dried medical herbs giving off sometimes sweet and sometimes stomach-turning scents, and everywhere cabbages seemed to be for sale. Chinese families huddled outside of a shrine, poking burning incense sticks into giant bronze cauldrons filled with sand and bowing three times before entering.

Su led me to a corner of the temple grounds where a large tent of tan canvas stood. A black lacquered signboard with the Chinese characters "求籤" painted in gold leaned beside its open entry flaps. I didn't recognize those characters — of course, I probably only knew a few hundred. Whatever they meant, apparently, they advertised something inside. A young man practically danced out of the tent with a huge grin, spoke to a young woman waiting, and then the two hurried off. But that didn't really tell me much about what went on inside.

"Where are we, Su? You think they brought Papa here?"

"No. But since we don't know where to start, maybe we can get some celestial help." She pointed to the sign. "See those characters? 'Ch'iu ch'ien,' that's what it says. This is a traditional Chinese fortune teller who uses little wooden sticks to make predictions."

"We'll get a clue using sticks, Su? Are you serious?"

"Lucy, you'll have to trust me on this one, okay? Let's give it a try. It won't take long." She dug out a few coins from her pocket. "Just remember, he will guide you, but I cannot guarantee he will give you the answers you want."

I peeked into the dim room. A man sat at an octagonal table facing the entrance. He was still, almost motionless, like an ancient oak tree, old and rough and lined, yet somehow still sturdy. His wispy beard brushed the tabletop.

"Who is that? He looks half dead!"

"Shhhhhh! Wait," Su hissed. A map was pinned to the tent wall. It resembled a star chart, but with many Chinese characters and other symbols, and lines connecting the various stars and planets in a dizzying pattern. On the table rested a large, weathered book which must have been written generations ago, with a bamboo cup holding dozens of slender sticks beside it.

The fortune teller cast his eyes upon me and beckoned us in with a wrinkled hand. "Come in, come in."

I gripped Su's arm. Strangely, though outside there was a great commotion, inside the tent it was ghostly silent, as if we had crossed over into some other world.

"How may I help you?"

The fortune teller's face was unreadable, but I could sense his surprise. I doubt he had many big-nose customers.

24

"Lucy, tell him about what happened with your father," Su said. The fortune teller craned his head forward, straining to comprehend my thick accent. As I told the story, Su filled in details with Chinese words I did not know.

He wrinkled his face in concentration as Su posed questions I couldn't follow. When she'd finished, the fortune teller's milky gray eyes, until now glazed over like he was only half awake, popped open. Suddenly animated though a moment ago he was drowsy, he went on and on asking questions. When at last he stopped, he handed me the bamboo cup of sticks.

"Why do they have numbers on them?" I asked.

"Each of those sticks corresponds to a piece of ancient writing." Su motioned towards the large book on the table. "All written in there. Fate decrees which stick comes out. The fortune teller uses the number to look up the oracle in his book. He interprets the meaning of the oracle, which then gives clues about the future."

"Shake it," the fortune teller ordered, clearly growing impatient with my curiosity.

The once-light cup suddenly felt heavy in my hands, as if someone had dropped a piece of lead in the bottom while I wasn't looking. It took all my strength to rattle the sticks, their collisions creating a noise like a lion's roar. Unconsciously Su stepped back, startled by the violent noise erupting from the cup. Clearly, I was not just imagining it. Well, I figured these were all just a magician's tricks, like pulling a rabbit from a hat. But I'd see it through. I flicked my hand and a stick soared out, slapping the table as it came to rest on its surface.

"Seventeen," declared the fortune teller, and he nodded and reached for his book. Each page crackled as he turned it until he found the corresponding entry for number seventeen. As he read, he stroked his chin, deep in thought.

"Well, what does it mean?" Su asked.

"You." The fortune teller looked up suddenly at Su and grinned as if he had just stumbled on the solution of a vexing problem. "*You* must also cast one of the sticks."

"Me?"

"You are a part of this as well. So the oracles reveal," the fortune teller replied.

"Go ahead, Su." She took the cup, shook it, this time prepared for the lion's roar of noise. She flicked and released one of the sticks. It landed on the table: twenty-three.

Once again, the fortune teller consulted his book, his brow knit until he finished. He closed the volume and then moved about the tent at a glacial speed, face creased in concentration. At last he turned up a scroll and unrolled it. "Yes, this is the one," he muttered to himself, then took his seat again, spread the scroll on the table and began poring over it.

Naturally curious, Su leaned in, examining the long columns of faded, ancient-looking Chinese characters.

"No peeking!" the fortune teller harrumphed at her, then he rolled the scroll up again. He closed his eyes. He was so lost in thought it looked like he might never find his way back again.

"What's he doing?" I whispered to Su.

"I have no idea."

Opening, the fortune teller's eyes did the weird popping thing again and he glanced at me. "A...bird?"

"Wh-what?" I stammered.

"After your father disappeared, was there something relating to a bird?"

I was so thunderstruck it took me half a minute to respond. For the first time, I saw this as maybe something more than a stage-magic show. "Um, yes. I found this."

In the dimness of the tent, the Firebird feather seemed to throw off a crimson glow when I drew it out. Staring at it a long

26

while, the old man consulted his book and then said, "If you find the bird this feather came from, you will be reunited with your father."

"How do we do that? I have no idea where this bird is or even what it looks like!" I exclaimed.

"There is much that remains unknown to me, but not all has stayed hidden. Your father is far from here, several days' journey, across lands where the forgotten creatures still walk, but for not much longer."

I was about to pepper him with questions, but Su motioned me to silence. Brow furrowed, he continued consulting the book until he added, "The two shall guide you, like *yin* and *yang*, but the five shall oppose you. This, I am sure, means the *wu hsing*: fire, wood, water, earth, metal." The old man turned grave. "I do not know exactly what this message holds, but each of these will pose danger."

He pored over the text some more, and I took advantage of the moment to whisper to Su. "What's the wu hsing?"

"The Five Chinese Elements. They are what matter is made of, according to traditional thinking. They have complicated relationships with one another. For example, wood feeds fire, because it burns, but it also overcomes earth."

"Why would it overcome earth?"

Just then the old man finished reading from his book. "Your father, he is held against his will in a strong, protected place. Almost impossible to enter."

Su and I exchanged an overwhelmed glance. "This protected place," she asked, "do you have any idea where it might be?"

The fortune teller flipped through his book again. "Past a dark and sprawling forest."

"But that could be anywhere," said Su.

Again, the fortune teller reviewed the entries in the book, and then scratched his chin, seemingly as confused by the answers as his customers. "You must seek help from the man ... one who cannot die."

My stomach dropped. While this was surely perplexing to the fortune teller, I knew immediately who he was referring to. "Can you tell us anything more? Anything at all?" I begged but he said nothing else. We thanked him and stumbled out of the tent.

6

The Lie

Su grabbed my arm, yanking me in front of her. "Listen to me, Lucy. I know what you are thinking, and you mustn't do it."

"Oh, are you a fortune teller now, too? Can you read minds of all those around you?"

"Only yours, dear friend." She was right, I was already planning my next steps. "And if you think that I will sit by and let you wander into the mouth of that beast, Vlad, you don't really know me."

"But didn't you hear what the fortune teller said about the man who can't die?"

"I did, and that is why I am telling you to head straight home, you understand?"

"Su, I think you're overreacting. I've met the man already."

"There are things you don't comprehend, that you cannot see. Have you ever been to the Badlands before?"

"No. Have you?"

She looked as if I'd just asked whether she'd like to dive into a pile of horse manure. "Certainly not. There are parts of this city where I just don't belong — and neither do you!"

"I don't care where I belong!"

Su looked like she was about to stamp her foot on the ground, her fiery temper barely contained. But she kept control of herself and simply said, "We will go, I promise. But we need a plan first.

What good will it do your father if you go to the Badlands and never come out again? I must work now or I'll lose my job, and *my* father needs that money. I'll come up with something and we'll go tomorrow. No searching the Badlands for your man who won't die—not without me. Okay?"

I nodded disingenuously. I dared not tell her the truth that nothing would stop me searching for my father this instant—even if it meant lying to my best friend. We walked towards the temple gateway in silence and as we exited to the street, Su pointed to the right. "That is the way home. Go!"

I walked a little way down the street and turned around to see Su watching me like a hawk, making sure I didn't change direction. I wasn't appreciating her newfound bossy streak, though I knew it was how she expressed her worry for me. Despite her good intentions, what Su couldn't understand was that such places as the Badlands don't scare me like she thinks. When I escaped St Petersburg, I saw terrible things, memories I can only revisit in my nightmares when all I see is blood-red snow. Turning around again, I saw Su was gone. Without a moment's hesitation I pivoted and made my way west, towards Vlad the Deathless.

I walked to Ch'ienmen and passed through that giant gatehouse and then the crowds of Dashilar, this time staying wide of the spitting camels. Reaching the intersection, I looked across the road down the empty street leading into the Badlands— empty because people of good sense kept far away from where it led. And when I saw the Taotie symbol painted on the wall, I hesitated. Reaching into my coat pocket, I felt the feather. "*I will swim across rivers, I will chase leopards and sneak past sleeping tigers, I will even track the Firebird through the forest, if I must...*" Papa's words from his letter echoed in my mind, and next thing I knew, my feet were crossing the road.

The empty street wound along until joining the main thoroughfare of the Badlands. The rundown hovels and shacks were just as you'd expect from residents who gave little thought to tomorrow. Here the people had a rougher look to them, too. Some had a thinly veiled fierceness, like caged animals eagerly seeking an opportunity to break out and attack. Others seemed as if they were merely sleepwalking, their sluggish eyes barely registering what was in front of them. The twilight gloom falling on the streets intensified the already sordid character of the neighborhood.

For half an hour I wandered around, pretending I knew exactly where I was going, even when I bumbled into blind alleys and had to turn around again. I don't know what I had been imagining, but somehow, I thought finding Vlad's place would be easier and started thinking I ought to have listened to Su.

The streets grew busier and I heard all sorts of languages and accents. There was Chinese, English, and maybe Mongolian, Korean, Japanese, German. Within that stew of tongues, some familiar words bubbled up to my ears.

Russian!

It came from a group of men huddling outside a ramshackle house that looked as if a stiff wind might knock it over. A haunted, far-away look hung over the men, like they were ghosts lost in the daylight, but one gazed at me not unkindly. He leaned against the gray concrete wall, his threadbare Russian army coat dwarfing his thin frame and suggesting he was once a man of great strength. Now he looked like a boy playing dress-up with his father's clothes. He gave me a weary smile as I approached.

"A proper Russian lady in these parts," he said. "Now that's something I never thought I'd see." He lit a cigarette.

"I'm looking for someone. Can you help me?" I was glad to see that buried in a scoundrel's face twinkled a pair of kind eyes.

"Depends. Ordinarily I'd ask what you will pay for this information." He studied me, even noticing my worn-out shoes. "But I see you are nearly as luckless as I am. Well, you'll have to tell me more before I can decide. A name might be a start." He smirked and released a huge smoke ring into the murky gray night.

"Vlad the Deathless. Do you know him?"

He whistled and chuckled in disbelief. "My Czarina, you are a funny one." He sighed. "Most people are trying to hide from The Deathless, not the other way around."

"He has some information I urgently need. Where can I find him?" He gave me a quizzical look, trying to weigh whether to tell. "Please. My father, he was a soldier like you. He's missing and Vlad might know where to find him."

He kept me waiting so long I thought he might have fallen asleep, but at last he replied, "Look for the brick building at the end of the lane." He gestured to his left. "The one that is the color of blood. That's where you'll find your man."

I thanked him and walked off to the left. Just as I turned the corner, he yelled after me, "I warn you, Czarina, make no deals with that man — or you'll regret it."

I could hear his hollow chuckle trailing behind me. The day was darkening, though it was only now that the neighborhood was slowly waking, yawning, as if taking a morning stretch. I saw a tall building at the end of the block and, boy, that Russian was right, it was as red as my nightmares. It stood three stories tall and looked as solid as a fortress or prison. Iron bars spanned the windows, from which escaped jazzy music, men's excited voices and a curious click-clacking.

As I approached, the strong metal door swung open. A hulking, tuxedoed Chinese with a face of stone shoved a skinny man through the doorway. "You can't throw me out, not when I was just about to win! Let me back in!" pleaded the gambler, but the hulk slammed the door in his face.

As I stood across the street looking straight at it, I came to a disturbing realization: I had no idea what to do once I got in. And even before that, with the doorman on guard, getting in was no sure thing. I couldn't just knock and ask to see Vlad, as if arriving for a tea party. I could hear Su's angry voice scolding me for my stupidity. I took a deep breath, remembering what Papa used to tell me. "If you are scared of wolves, don't go in the woods." You can only lose from fear, never gain. And when Papa's life hung in the balance, fear was not a luxury I could afford.

7

THE GAMBLE

I waited, watching. Gamblers came and gamblers went, along with their fortunes. The doorman never strayed from his post and I made sure to stay hidden from his sight behind a large column. A horse-drawn wagon, stuffed with wooden crates, turned the corner and pulled up in front of the casino. The Chinese peasant driving waved to the doorman. I strained to hear the conversation, but fortunately, both men's voices did not dip below a yell.

"I got everything he asked for," the driver said.

"You're certain?"

"I think so. Want me to unload it here?"

"No, it stays in the wagon. And put it around back."

"How do I get there?"

"Turn down the second hutong on the right."

"Over there?"

"No, no, that one dead-ends. The other one." Grumbling, the doorman came down the stairs and walked up to the driver. If ever I had a chance, it was now. As he pointed out the directions, I bolted from my spot, going wide of the wagon, and then crept along the street back towards the entrance. Just before the doorman turned, I raced up the stairs and plunged into the casino.

I had to chop through the low-hanging, smoky air, thick as

a blizzard on the steppes. Men, Chinese and foreign, leered like devils at their games of chance. What an assortment of deadbeats, each looking more desperate and untrustworthy than the next. Some sat at tables covered in green felt. Others played cards and rolled dice. The click-clacking was the sound of colorful *mahjong* tiles being slammed onto the tables by excited players. It was a game a little like cards, which sometimes people played in the streets, too. I walked over towards the back, where several men huddled around a table enclosed by walls, like a miniature arena. Two crickets wrestled at the center of the felt battleground, while the men gathered around, yelled frenziedly and placed bets with each other. The fight went on several moments, until one cricket surrendered and the winner stalked to the corner, beating its wings in victory. The owner of the defeated cricket shoved it into a tiny rattan basket in his shirt pocket and stomped off.

There was no sign of Vlad the Deathless, though along the back wall I spotted a narrow flight of stairs leading to the second floor. My only hope was that he might be up there. I pushed my way over, climbed the first step — then a hand heavy as a block of stone fell on my shoulder.

"Lost, are we?" asked the doorman. A wide face framed his fierce eyes. He began ushering me towards the door. I stopped and felt his grip tighten as I turned towards him. "Sir, I need to speak with Vlad!" I pleaded. "It's very important!"

He paused for a moment, gave me what I thought was a pitying look — and shoved me in the direction of the door. I dug my heels into the floor, once again. "Come on, little girl, you can walk out — or I'll throw you out." He put his hand on my back and pushed, which felt like a bulldozer driving me forward.

"All right, all right," I said, walking toward the door until I felt his hand move away from me — then I spun and dashed back for the stairs. He lunged, grabbing a bit of my jacket, but

I twisted and got free of him. Diving under a long card table, I crawled across the gamblers' feet, peering out and seeing the doorman's tree-trunk legs running to the end of the table nearest the back stairs, I suppose because he guessed I would come there. Instead I crawled out on the side, getting to my feet as he hurried to intercept me. I spied an empty chair nearby so I sprang onto it then landed on a mahjong table, scattering the tiles every which way as I ran across, leaving an echo of angry voices behind me.

From that table I leaped into the cricket-fighting arena and almost lost my balance when I landed because I had to make an awkward move so I didn't squash any of those tiny insect warriors. The gamblers were in an uproar, and the doorman was trying to push them aside to reach me when I jumped down and darted up the stairs. The doorman's heavy footsteps pounded right behind me.

I reached the office door and just as I gripped the knob, a gigantic arm closed around me. It was like being wrapped in the arms of a bear. "Let me go! Let me go, please! I *must* speak to Vlad!" Ignoring my screams of protest, the doorman hauled me back down the stairs.

"What's all this infernal ruckus?" a voice boomed at the top of the stairs.

I squirmed in the doorman's arms and gazed up at a sleek, elegant figure in a dapper gray suit and gleaming black shoes. The Deathless. We stood there for a moment, gazing at each other, unsure who was the more surprised. He looked past me to the gamblers gathered at the foot of the stairs, some chirping at me in surprise, others irate I'd ruined their hands at the tables, but all were staring up at us, awaiting his judgment of me. He frowned a moment, then grinned so subtly, if I'd blinked at that moment, I'd have missed it.

"It is all right, Chen. This little bird has simply strayed too far from her nest," he said in his flawless Chinese. "Let her go." The muscleman released me. Switching seamlessly back to Russian, Vlad said, "Well, come on now. After the trouble you've gone to seeing me, it would be very impolite to not offer you tea."

Vlad beckoned me up. Instantly I felt like I'd traveled thousands of miles, and back in time. The rich aroma of black tea and antique mustiness, with a hint of frankincense, scented the air. On the wall hung religious icons adjacent to oil paintings of the Russian countryside. A huge samovar for making tea was almost a twin of the one I had growing up, decorated in an elaborate mosaic pattern and standing nobly in a corner. This room was the closest place to my homeland I had seen since I'd left.

"Though I'm intrigued and perhaps, impressed with your nerve, I daresay working my customers up into a froth is not exactly excellent for business."

His Russian was surprisingly courtly. It was the sort of language I expected of characters in my storybooks, easily understandable to me yet still conjuring a far-off time of castles and wintry rides in a *troika*, a Russian sleigh. Certainly not the tone of speech I expected of a gangster.

Vlad sat down behind his large wooden desk and lit a long cigarette. He looked almost like a dragon as the smoke drifted around his scarred face. Somehow, he appeared a tad older than at the train station, like he'd aged three years in a day. Perhaps he, too, had heavier thoughts ever since then.

"Please, sit." He motioned me towards a plush sofa, then selected two tea glasses from a shelf. He dropped a cherry in each and filled them with steaming tea from the samovar. When he presented the drink on a silver tray, I saw the glasses bore etchings of dramatic forest scenes.

The tea was a perfect concoction of bitter and sweet. "This

tastes just like home!" I blurted.

"That's because it *is* Russian tea! Every week I have it delivered from Moscow. Even in times of war, a gentleman needs proper tea." I wasn't particularly sold on the gentleman part, though I did enjoy the tea.

"But the war is over, my father told me so."

"Don't fool yourself. It is never over. War has no home. It just slips from place to place like a traveling salesman peddling an endless supply of misery."

A silence settled as we sipped our tea.

"Hmm." Vlad leaned back in his chair, deep in thought. He motioned to the large painting behind him showing a fearsome wolf in a woodland. "What do you think when you look at that creature?"

I supposed this was some kind of test, and I spoke hesitantly. "Well, at first I think he looks a bit scary because he is baring his teeth. But he is also... beautiful. He reminds me of the wolf from the story of Prince Ivan and the Firebird. At first, he is unkind because he kills Prince Ivan's poor horse, but then he allows the prince to ride him, and even rescues him from trouble."

He favored me with an enigmatic smile. "Yes indeed, the Firebird!"

"You know that story?"

"Intimately. As does every true Russian."

I drew out my feather. "Then you would know this?"

"Where did you find that?" Vlad suddenly bolted upright and stared as if hypnotized at the feather. "You must tell me everything."

I told him the whole story, from seeing him at the train station, to the consultation with the fortune teller. He reached for another cigarette. "Ah, yes, I remember you now. I thought you looked familiar. I was understandably distracted by the abduction of my horse, who was making the trip from Russia to join me. But I fail to see why you are in need of my assistance." After lighting another cigarette, he leaned back in his chair once again, his beady eyes still cemented to the feather.

"I've heard you know where the warlord lives. The Taotie."

"That I may. A rough sense, anyhow. Though he has an army, with cannons, guns and thousands of cut-throats. I wouldn't recommend a social call."

Hearing now the same sort of warning from Vlad as from Su, I felt a temptation to just shrink away in defeat. *Of course*, there was nothing that I, a twelve-year-old refugee in a foreign land, could do about my father's abduction by a notorious warlord. But all the same, there was something else gathering in my soul, my love for Papa twinned with outrage that he could be taken from me—that could not be denied.

"You must understand, sir, that my father, he is all I have left now. For three years we have been apart."

Vlad looked indifferent. "In my time I've heard many sad tales."

"Help me, sir. Help someone from your part of the world."

"I shall tell you something, a piece of wisdom: sometimes it is wisest to accept what Fate has wrought."

At that I wanted to slap him. "Do you think I can actually let my father be a prisoner of that horrible man? And what about your horse? You will leave him to suffer at the hands of that monster?"

That landed, for Vlad winced. "Her, not him," he mumbled sadly. "Ah, my poor Dusha, I should never have left her side."

"Well, tell me where to go and I'll rescue her, too!" I went on, thinking I was about to persuade him. "But you will come too, right?"

He pursed his lips. "No."

"Fine. Where must I go, you can at least tell me that."

"No."

"Why not?"

"I do not concern myself with others' problems. Long, long ago I learned that lesson in a most decisive fashion. Now, Lucy, as deep a pleasure as it is sipping tea with you, business demands my attention." Vlad gestured to the door, his manners still impeccable but his meaning clear and firm.

I decided to gamble a little. "But it's not as if I am asking you to do something you aren't planning yourself. Only that you bring me along."

His eyes bored into me. "What is it I plan to do?"

"Find the warlord. And rescue your horse, I suppose."

"And why do you think that?"

"Well, that's what all those supplies out back are for, aren't they? In the wagon?"

There was a flicker of surprise in his eye, and perhaps grudging respect. "The wise gambler knows when to stop. The bold gambler knows when the only choice is to bet everything." He rose, gesturing to the door. "I salute your gamesmanship, Lucy, but you have no hand to play against me. Now off you go."

8

THE VISITOR

As I feared, posted at the front entrance of my house stood Su, and upon laying eyes on me, she marched over. Though the darkness concealed the rage on her face, I certainly felt its heat.

"I knew it! You went to the Badlands! I can smell it on you!"

I wondered if this was a Chinese saying, then sniffed my coat. It did reek of tobacco smoke from Vlad's casino.

"Su, what choice did I have?"

"You had plenty of choices, Lucy! Like waiting for me! But you chose the most dangerous one! You could have been kidnapped — or worse! Frankly, I'm surprised you are still alive!"

Neighbors began peering out of the windows to see what the commotion was all about.

"Stop shouting, you will wake up the whole neighborhood."

She pretended not to hear me. "Was it worth it, at least? Did that rotten gangster tell you anything useful?" She stepped closer with a challenging glare.

I lowered my voice to a forceful whisper. "He didn't seem especially keen on helping me." Immediately I turned away, not wanting to see the satisfied look on her face.

"Go tell Madam Korchigina you are home, she'll be worried." She spun and strode off.

I walked into the apartment where Korchigina was hovering over the sink. She looked over at me disapprovingly, then turned back to the dishes, before wiping her hands on the dishrag and shuffled towards the living room where I was sitting. "Do you think this is a hotel, where you can simply come and go as you please?"

I looked at my feet. "No." Another lecture—just what I needed.

"Louder!" she yelled.

I stared at her ruddy face. "NO, Ma'am!"

"Good, don't let that happen again." She walked away into the bedroom and I didn't have long to wait before her snores reached a rumbling crescendo. I tiptoed into the bedroom and crawled into my pallet. I just wanted to escape into sleep.

But it wouldn't come. Images of the day raced through my mind, the haunting faces of the Badlands, the wolf portrait, Vlad's steely eyes concentrating on my feather. But most of all, I thought of Papa, the terrible place where he must be trapped, and how I could do nothing to help him. I had failed him already.

I must have dozed off, because next I knew I was being violently shaken. For a moment, I thought I was having another one of my nightmares.

"Lucy, Lucy, wake up!" Su whispered harshly. She must have climbed in through the window.

"What's wrong?" I managed, the fear twisting her face chilling me more than the night air.

She pointed toward the street. "He's out there!"

"Who?" I asked, struggling to sit up.

"I told you, Lucy, you should never have gone to see him! He didn't like you poking into his business!"

It was still dark out, though dawn would be coming soon. Su probably saw whoever it was while on her way to martial-arts practice and then ran back to warn me. I crept to the window. A figure lurked in the shadows of the lane. All I could see was a reedy silhouette and the glowing whites of a man's eyes. Then he stepped out of the shadows and into the moonlight. I gasped.

It was Vlad, and he looked perfectly sinister. Yet somehow, I knew he was not here for the reasons Su thought. I opened the window.

Su gripped my arm. "What are you doing?!"

"Don't worry. He's come as a friend." Wriggling my arm free, I clambered out the window and dropped into the lane.

Vlad was dressed very differently now, in rougher clothing, with a brown cape and floppy, wide-brimmed black hat.

"There is no time to dawdle, hurry now!"

"What? Why are you here?" I asked.

"Is it not obvious? We both have things the Taotie must return."

"I thought you had no interest in helping me!"

"Well, maybe my conscience got the better of me. Or maybe I just need to rescue my horse, and some masochistic part of my character insists on bringing a useless girl along!"

"But wait, you're not here alone? Where are your men? Where's that ogre doorman of yours?"

"They will be of no use and only slow us down," Vlad snapped. "Now pack your things!"

Su came out to the alley. "Why do you think we'll even go with you?"

Vlad glanced over, seeing Su for the first time, and scanning her suspiciously. "And who are you?" he demanded. "I didn't know you were invited?"

"This is Su. My best friend," I answered.

Vlad stepped forward and scoured her with those creepy, knowing eyes of his. "Unwise. She cannot be trusted. A spy for the Taotie, most likely."

"Me? A spy?" Su fumed. Her feet shifted to a shoulder's width apart, just like they did when she was practicing her martial arts. I held her back.

"Why not? He pays well, that's what I hear. A poor girl with a sick father will do anything for money, eh?" Vlad glided towards her, staring her dead in the eye. I wondered how he knew about the poor health of Su's dad.

She lifted her chin and met his glare. "Why did you agree to do this? What's in it for you? And how do we know *you* won't betray *us*?"

"So many questions from one who knows nothing. Tell me, do we go this way?" He pointed a crooked finger to the east. "Or this way?" He pointed north. Su couldn't answer.

"Stop it!" I hissed at them both. "My trust should count for something."

"Lucy, how can you trust this criminal?" Su countered.

"I don't think you have much of a choice, my friend," Vlad said to me. "I have a pony, cart, and supplies. Not to mention I know where to go." He gestured down the street to a darkened doorway. "The Taotie's men have been watching you like hungry hawks. Did you know that?"

"What? Watching us? Why?"

"I suppose it is because if your father causes too much trouble, well, they will make you pay the price," he said to me. "If we leave at daybreak, it's too late. The Taotie will know we are coming."

Su looked doubtful. "How do you know they are watching?"

"The Taotie is not the only one with eyes all over the city."

A shiver ran down my spine. "Then what do we do about those men?"

"Fortunately, they are sleeping the night away now."

"How do you know they're actually asleep?" I walked down the street and saw two slumbering forms in the doorway — the

Russian and Chinese goons who had made trouble at the stinky bean curd shop.

"Because I did it to them," he announced, and before I could ask how, he added, "Now it's time we depart!"

I ran into my room and quickly changed out of my night clothes. I threw an old blue dress over my head and put on my coat, touching the Firebird feather still in its pocket. The house was quiet and still, the hubbub hadn't woken up the watcher Korchigina. Probably I should have left her a note, but I couldn't slow down even for that. I went to the street and climbed into the cart. Su got in right beside me.

"Hold on! You have a job, Su. And your father is here. You can't just leave. If you lose your job, what will happen?"

She pulled out a beautiful jade amulet from her pocket. It was a small smooth oval, the color of mint two days past its prime. It had an engraved character — 忠 — which she traced with her fingertip. "This."

"What does it mean?"

"Loyalty. And so does the jade it is carved upon. Now, my dear friend, you are in trouble, and it is my duty to help you. Fate will figure out the rest. Besides," she added with a grin, "do you honestly think I'd let you travel with this monster alone?"

I knew there was no use arguing with her. And even though I told her not to come, I was so relieved that she did.

The moment the wheels started to turn, I felt a sudden nagging feeling, a pulling. I realized what I'd forgotten. "Stop right up ahead. There is something I must get, one moment!"

Before Vlad could protest, I jumped out and scrambled up the tree, ran along the wall, came to the temple, and dropped inside. I don't know why I felt a need for it, but my bones told me so. I lifted the loose stone. Luba's head was sticking outside the top of her cotton pouch. Funny, I hadn't remembered leaving

THE PHOENIX AND THE FIREBIRD

her like that, but I was in such a hurry I didn't think much of it. I grabbed my doll, stuffing her into my coat pocket, next to the Firebird feather.

"Hurry up, you're slower than a blind owl at night," Vlad grumbled as I returned.

"Ready!" I yelled, running towards the cart. I grabbed Su's outstretched hand and she pulled me in.

9

THE DARKNESS

After an hour bumping along in the cart, the thick city walls rose ahead of us. We came to a gate leading out of Peking, its arches bringing both comfort and unease. Vlad stopped the cart at the threshold. He faced us both, looking terribly serious. "Once we pass through this gate, we are wandering into the shadowlands. Any safeguards we may have end here. Now is your last chance to turn back."

He was trying to protect us, but it frustrated me all the same. If there was one thing I hated, it was being underestimated. "Can't this thing go any faster?"

He jumped at my sudden biting tone, then grinned, shaking his head as he yelled, "Hyah, hyah!" to get the horse moving again. As we rode out of the city, the landscape opened to a grand expanse, the cramped, busy streets of the city quickly evaporating. There was some traffic on the road, most of it traveling against us, farmers and merchants heading to the city to sell their products. Seeing all their goods, I was struck with how unprepared I was for the journey. "Should we buy some supplies?" I asked Vlad.

He gestured to two large trunks in the rear of the wagon. "I have enough food and blankets so that even you two princesses shouldn't complain."

After some time traveling, the road traffic thinned and by

early afternoon, we could go ten minutes or more before another cart or person passed us. Vlad drove the wagon ever farther north, where we stopped seeing villages. There was little more than farmland. Su sat tranquilly, probably recalling or composing a poem in her head. She always says it is her way of thinking, reaching into her mind to find the correct verse for the moment. I was about to ask her which poem she was thinking about when her trance was broken by the smell of rot. Her body stiffened as she looked on decaying crops. "So much waste. These fields should have been harvested."

"The farmers have been run off by the Taotie. I wouldn't be surprised if he also made the boys and men serve in his army," Vlad said.

Su snorted, muttering, "Nasty, superstitious fool."

"Where does he come from?" I asked.

"No one knows," she said. "Many of these warlords, they were officers in the Imperial Army before it was dissolved. The Taotie just came from nowhere."

"Like magic?" I asked.

"If you want to call it that. Maybe black magic. Or like some monster."

"Like his name, yes?" Vlad said. "The taotie is a Chinese creature from some centuries ago."

"Yes," answered Su. "It was said to especially enjoy eating people, and greedy people tasted best of all." She gave a nod towards Vlad's turned back. "I was telling Lucy before they appear on some ancient cauldrons."

Vlad stroked his chin and turned to her. "I wonder what became of them."

"The cauldrons?" asked Su. "I saw one in a museum once." She still refused to look at Vlad directly; he would have to earn that. Instead she feigned a deep interest in studying the scenery.

"No, not the cauldrons—the taotie creatures," replied Vlad, without a hint of a smile. What an odd sense of humor, but then gangsters are not known for their hilarity. He turned away and focused on driving the wagon. Soon after, the wagon took a curve in the road and beside it stood the blackened remnants of a farming village. There was not a soul in sight, not a dog or a pig. Even the birds seemed to fly clear of it, as if the air were poisoned. Somberness hung over the place and the acrid odor of still-smoldering houses.

A crude wooden sign was posted at the mouth of the road leading into the village, with several characters carved into it. "What does that say, Su?"

She spoke in a hollow voice. "It says, this is what happens to those who defy the Taotie."

We rode on in silence as the sky was dimming and the broad, open road grew thin, its edges crowded by trees. Try as I might, I couldn't get that evil sign out of my head, and I felt as though the burnt village's bitter air trailed me like an ominous cloud. And I knew the closer we came to the Taotie's fortress, the greater the dangers we would face. I only hoped I would be ready for them.

Vlad pulled on the horse's reins. "Best we stop here. It's been a long day. And who knows what this forest holds for us?" He smiled, a smile I couldn't decide was friendly or sinister. You could never tell with him. He emptied the cart of blankets and food. He hadn't lied earlier, we were very well stocked, with noodles, Russian black bread, cheese, smoked bean curd, sacks of walnuts, dried fruit and more. This journey might bring many discomforts, but hunger ought not to be one of them.

"Gather wood and we'll have us a fire," Vlad growled as he attached a feedbag to the horse's head.

"Gather it where?" I asked, hoping he didn't mean the darkening forest.

"Where do you think, silly girl?" He chortled, nodding towards the wood.

As I picked kindling, I couldn't help feeling the leafless tree limbs above resembled knobby witch's fingers ready to snatch me at any moment. Su had wandered out of sight, and I had to fight the temptation to scream her name. But what did I really have to be afraid of other than the darkness? My fear seemed sensible, though, as I gazed into the depths of the forest, my eyes swallowed by its blackness. I experienced a strange sensation no words could easily describe. This was a place, I sensed somewhere down deep in me, like no other. The closest I could think of was the woodland scene with a wolf in Vlad's painting, something menacing and wild, but tinged with beauty and the adventurous possibilities of the unknown.

With shaking hands I picked up as much kindling as I could and hurried back to the campsite. There was no sign of Su yet. Vlad had set out a blanket and was building a ring of stones for our fire pit.

"Ah, she returns! I worried the *belushka* might have become lost in the forest."

The breath went out of me as though I had just jumped into an icy lake. *Belushka*—"Little Squirrel" in Russian. It was my father's nickname for me. How did Vlad know this? There was no way that he could, perhaps it was just a coincidence. After all, squirrels *do* live in the forest. Yet I knew this was no fluke.

"Why did you use that name for me?"

Vlad kept arranging the kindling in the fire pit. "Belushka, you mean?"

"Yes."

"That is what you remind me of, a little squirrel. You have big eyes, with a glimmer of trouble."

"That is my father's nickname for me."

"Ha! It must be a very accurate one, then!"

"Perhaps so." I shrugged, not quite convinced, but my unease lightened when Su returned with an armful of sticks and kindling. She set it all down beside the pit and Vlad built a fire.

"Are there any matches in these bags?" I asked him.

Su dug into a pocket but Vlad said, "No need." He reached deep into the stacked kindling, then yanked his hands out. Flames burst from the stacked wood as if it was a firecracker, causing Su and I to leap back.

"How did he do that?!" exclaimed Su, her awe making her temporarily forget how much she disliked the man.

Vlad grabbed a loaf of black bread from his bag and tore off great chunks which he tossed to Su and me like he was feeding ducks in a pond. I was too hungry to care and stuffed the bread in my mouth. I had not realized how famished I'd become. I stuffed myself so much that I couldn't even finish and placed a scrap of bread in my coat pocket beside Luba. Vlad, though, reclining on an elbow, only nibbled, uninterested in his food. No wonder he was looking, with each passing hour it seemed, more and more like a skeleton.

After finishing her food, Su grew squirmy. Ordinarily she held herself still, but I could tell she craved her daily exercise. "I'll be back in a few minutes," she announced, and off she went, starting her routine of punches and kicks within a grove of pine trees nearby.

Vlad glanced over at me and spoke in our language. "Your accent, it is St. Petersburg, yes? The most beautiful city in the world, I say." I nodded. "I've been there a few times on business. But I imagine it has changed since then."

"Well, everywhere has changed back there," I said. "Where is your home? In Russia, I mean."

"Hmm, not an easy question. I have been a traveler all my

days, or at least those I still remember. It is a bit like asking a fish in the sea. What is its home? 'Wherever there is water,' it might answer. I have rested my head in too many places to count. Let's say, my home is wherever Russian is spoken."

"Oh, that doesn't mean anything at all!" I snapped. I wasn't in the mood for riddles and metaphorical answers.

Chuckling at my outburst, Vlad looked me straight in the eye. "Well, if home is where your heart is fullest, then we shall call the forest my home."

"The forest?" I asked, perplexed.

"Why? Is that strange to you?"

"Um, yes, it *is* strange," I replied. "People are not of the forest. A village maybe, or a town, but not the forest, especially not this kind." To stress my point, I gestured towards the dark mass engulfing the entire horizon.

"Cities, they are wondrous in their own way," Vlad said, "though if you are not careful, the buildings become like jail cells. In the forest, you are always free."

"Anyway, you live in the city now." Maybe I shouldn't have been pushing so hard. I knew Vlad's temper could flare at any moment.

"That is true," he said, the lilt in his voice showing amusement at my frankness. "Well, you know as well as I that we've all had to adjust to our new circumstances. Russia does not want me anymore and I've had to make the best of my new life, regardless of how detestable some might find it." Vlad peered meaningfully at me.

I did know about people of the collapsed Russian Empire adjusting to new realities. We were like fallen apples, no longer able to return to the branches of our tree, nobody wanted anything to do with us as we were bruised and damaged. So we just rotted on the ground, waiting to disappear into the soil. It was strange to share this vulnerability with someone like Vlad. It made me uncomfortable that somehow such a man would make me feel less lonely. I could tell Su about how my father valiantly went to fight for the Czar, the emperor of Russia, how the war went badly, how most of my family was killed or sent far away to places like China or France, but she wouldn't understand. Not really. Although her family and so many others were driven from their privileged positions in society, and although they suffered deep humiliation, she still has a country, even if it is no longer what it was. Many of the people of the Empire now in China were once wealthy in their homeland, and they bemoan the loss of their jewels and grand parties. I must say I feel the sting of such losses too, robbed of our grand house, holidays in Crimea, beautiful clothes and an endless supply of books. Yet most of all, I missed having a country to call home. I was no longer a citizen of anywhere. I was stateless.

Su returned from her workout, surprised, I could tell, to detect the change in mood. Despite attempts at small talk, we were unable to blow off the fog of melancholy settling on us. Only the crackle of the fire and the low drone of insects competed with the silence. Until I heard another sound, a faint humming. I looked at Vlad, but he only stared into the fire. And Su gazed at the night sky, her mind clearly at work — perhaps composing a poem about the glistening stars watching us. But the humming kept growing louder and soon I recognized the tune.

"Is that 'Kalinka'?"

Vlad winked at me. His humming grew louder, more insistent.

"Kalinka" was a light-hearted folk song I heard all the time in St. Petersburg, but not once since then. Now its sound was like a strange medicine for my nerves, the terrors of the forest ebbing. As if summoned to it, I couldn't stop myself from singing:

THE PHOENIX AND THE FIREBIRD

"Little red berry, red berry, red berry of mine!
In the garden there's a berry – little raspberry,
raspberry of mine!
Ah, under the pine, the green one,
Lay me down to sleep,
Oh-swing, sway, Oh-swing, sway,
Lay me down to sleep."

I sang the verses again and again, each round faster than the last. Vlad clapped his hands, brightly cackling at the frenzied crescendos, and Su clapped along even though she couldn't understand the Russian lyrics. With each clap, the black mood that had weighed on our shoulders began to lift. Now Vlad danced. He twirled and galloped, whipped and leaped even more gracefully than a stallion. He was the finest dancer I had ever seen. Soon tears streamed down my face.

The song ended as if by unconscious consensus and we all flopped exhausted on the blanket. I wiped my face again, hoping the darkness hid my tears.

"Ash, the favorite song of soldiers!" Vlad sighed, his rail-thin body propped up by an elbow once again. "Reminds them of Mother Russia, always."

As Vlad rested, I thought about Mother Russia. That vast swath of land that was once under the rule of the Czars. I'd been young when I left, so my memories were not extensive, and, except for getting scolded by Madam Korchigina, I spoke the language rarely. It was strange that this gangster had become a link to my ancestral land, and stranger still – and alarming – how much I was coming to enjoy his company.

I could hear Vlad's heavy inhalations as he tried to catch his breath, winded from the feverish dancing. Then I heard another sound mingling in, and I couldn't place it. A strange scraping sound. And bells, gently tinkling bells.

Vlad reached for the knife on his belt and placed a finger to his lips indicating we should stay silent. Now there resolved a figure shambling toward us. It must have been the darkness playing tricks, for it looked like an overweight, strangely proportioned man. Not quite what I would expect to emerge from the forest in the middle of the night.

He stepped into the light of the fire.

10

THE WALKER

It was a young man, his body corded with muscle. With his trousers rolled up past his knees, I could see his calves which looked like massive blocks of marble. On his back rode an old man with a wispy white beard, a pale face and his eyes clamped deeply in slumber.

"Who... what is he doing?" I whispered to Su.

"What do you mean?" She didn't seem at all disturbed by the sight before us.

"For goodness' sake, there is a man strapped to his back!" I whispered.

"Yes, of course. A dead man. How else would he carry him?"

"*What*? A *dead* man?"

"Oh, you mean you've never seen one?" Su asked, almost as surprised at this as I was at the sight of a corpse on a man's back.

"One what?" I asked. Vlad looked over at Su attentively.

"Hello there!"

Before Su could answer, a cheerful voice beat her to it. We looked over to see two sets of hands waving at us. Despite his obvious exhaustion the young man was jolly. Su greeted him as he — they — came closer.

"I heard the most unusual singing. I was going to walk the other way, thinking it might be evil spirits trying to tempt me, but if they were, they would sing in Chinese and much better, I'd think. But oh my, I am so happy to see other people, even if they look a bit strange," he said, glancing at me and Vlad. He giggled, his huge smile a crazy contrast with the expressionless face of the dead man slouched behind him.

"They are foreigners," Su explained. The corpse-walker nodded in our direction with a sheepish grin.

"Would you care to rest by our fire?" Vlad offered in his near-fluent Chinese.

"Thank you." With gingerly movements which this stranger had obviously done so many times it became as natural as any of us taking a seat, he lowered himself onto a rock. He held his hands to the fire and smiled, oblivious to the expressions of shock and dismay on our faces. "Zhou, that's my name."

We introduced ourselves, and Zhou the corpse-walker complimented us foreigners on our Chinese.

"I can't stay long but it's nice to have a chat. I've got to get this guy to Peking by morning." He patted the ancient man's arm as if he was an old friend.

"Why are you going there?"

"That's where his family is. But he died five days' walk that way." He pointed in the direction opposite of the city.

"You've been walking around that long with a dead man tied to your back?" Now *that* was a sentence I never thought I'd speak.

"Yes. This time, it's not too bad. Sometimes it takes me weeks to get my customers home. And if it's summertime, the heat... " He waved his fingers in front of his nose, and Su giggled. I couldn't imagine hauling around a dead body under any conditions, but those sounded unimaginably awful, like something that might feature in the wickedest Russian fairytales.

"Customers? But how can they be customers when they're dead?" Vlad asked.

"Well, to be precise, their families are customers, but I like to think I'm providing one last service to the ones on my back."

My confusion only deepened. "But why do you walk? Couldn't you take a train or ride a cart?"

Zhou looked at me like these were the oddest questions. "Walking keeps the body from stiffening. That way they're a little bit more like the way their families remembered them. Besides, it wouldn't be polite to throw them in a cart or a wheelbarrow like they're a dead dog or something. No," he sniffed, "not polite at all."

Zhou didn't seem inclined to share much more about his profession. Instead, he stretched out and smiled like a contented emperor. "It sure is nice meeting you folks. Lonely nights out here, and there isn't a corpse-walker inn anywhere."

"A corpse-walker's inn — what's that?" I asked.

"Just what it sounds like. No one likes having us stay in regular inns, for, um, obvious reasons. So there are special ones just for walkers and their customers. But there's none in this area. There's hardly anything but forest and ghosts and bandits, though they're hardly the worst things out here."

I tried to imagine an inn with such clientele, what it might look like and I conjured many questions. When they sleep, do the walkers lay their corpses next to their beds? Was there a sort of 'corpse storeroom' for the strange cargo? And so on, each question more macabre than the next.

"Where did you come from?" asked Su.

"Near the Phoenix Mountain on the other side of the forest."

"That's where we're going," Vlad said.

That was the first I'd heard of this Phoenix Mountain. "How can we get there?" I asked the corpse-walker.

"Oh, well, there are two routes, technically. But only one route, really."

"What do you mean?" wondered Su.

"You can take the main road or cut through the forest. Most people take the road if they are sensible, though it takes a few days more."

"What's so bad about the forest?" I asked.

"Nothing—as long as you don't mind ending up like my customer here. Between the warlord's men and the forest spirits, few manage to come out again."

"You came out of the forest all right," Su observed.

"Sure I did. This," he patted the body behind him, "this is my armor. Nobody wants to disrupt the dead, not even the forest spirits. If I were just giving a living person a piggyback ride, now that would be another story. No, I wouldn't dare go into that forest without him."

"The forest spirits?" I asked skeptically.

"Yes, more than you can count. A haunted place that is, believe me." I glanced at Su, who shrugged. Vlad, busy tending the fire, seemed uninterested in this talk. No doubt such superstition was silly to a man of the underworld.

"Well, I should be going," said Zhou. "Like I said, I have to deliver this body by morning and frankly, before long he is going to start.... " He pinched his nose, as if he didn't want to hurt the corpse's feelings by implying it might soon start stinking.

Zhou tried to rise to his feet. 'Rats!' Again and again the corpse's weight kept pulling him back to the log as he tried to get up, truly a scene of black comedy. Finally Su helped hoist him to his feet.

"Thank you, young lady. Well, I'm off." He turned, looking directly at me. "Remember, stick to the road."

We waved goodbye and watched him hobble away, the corpse's feet dragging behind him, the bells jingling softer and softer until there was only the sound of the night.

11

THE CHOICE

As soon as Zhou was out of sight, Vlad rose to his feet. "I'm going to feed the horse." Before he left, he looked at me with an inscrutable expression, something between scorn and, somehow, encouragement. A peculiarly Russian sort of expression. He abruptly walked away from the fire and vanished before I could pin down what he was getting at.

"All right, I think we'd better get some sleep," Su said. "We have a long day tomorrow."

Sleep seemed remote, for I was wound up from what we had just learned. "Shouldn't we discuss what the corpse-walker told us?"

"Huh? What is there to discuss?" Su asked.

"Well, we need to decide which way to go."

She looked at me puzzled. "What do you mean? Obviously, we're taking the road."

"What? No, we can't—if we do, we'll never make it to Papa in time."

"Lucy, I understand, but the forest is too dangerous. We'll leave early tomorrow and ride all day. I bet we can make it to the warlord's castle even sooner than the corpse-walker said it would take. Remember, he is traveling with a dead man on his back."

"No, Su. You've got to listen to me. The corpse-walker said

ALEXIS KOSSIAKOFF & SCOTT FORBES CRAWFORD

the forest path is faster than the road. Much faster. The longer the warlord has Papa, the more danger he's in. We have to get to him as soon as we can!"

"What do you know about the forest, Lucy?" asked Su. "You are a city girl. So am I. We'd probably get lost in three minutes."

"We have Vlad with us. He knows the forest!"

Su raised her eyebrows. "And how do we know that gangster is not going to leave us the first chance he gets?" She swiveled her head to check he wasn't in earshot. "Lucy, you like to think the best of people, but now is the time for good judgment. Seeing things as they are. Don't you think it strange he would help two girls like us? You aren't the least bit suspicious? What does *he* get out of this?"

"Maybe he feels happy to be helping, doing something good for a change." I hoped it came off better than it sounded, for even to me it was feeble.

Grabbing my arm, Su pulled me close, her fierce eyes boring straight into mine. "Don't think that man does anything that does not benefit him in the end. It is not a matter of *if* he'll abandon us, only *when*. And frankly, Lucy, I'd rather not be in the middle of the forest when that happens."

I didn't respond, I just turned away, lying down on the blanket and slipping my hand into my coat pocket. As my fingertips brushed the doll's hair, a strange feeling of ... *knowing* ... came over me. I felt for the quill of the feather, its sharp tip a reminder of the dangers ahead. In my heart, somehow, in a way I could never really describe, I knew the road would be too slow and that if we chose it, I'd be too late to rescue Papa. And something more than that. Not only Papa, but many other people would suffer at the hands of the warlord unless we took the forest path. I shut my eyes, hoping I could escape into dreams, far away from my fears.

A little hungry again, I reached into my pocket for the scrap of bread I'd put there earlier. Where was it? I pulled out Luba and patted around but there was no sign of it except for a few crumbs on Luba's face. Oh well, maybe some bugs crawled in and stole the bread.

I must have fallen asleep, for I awoke to the dappling sunlight through the trees above. Su still peacefully slumbered under the blanket beside me. Vlad busily loaded the cart. He moved with purpose and an urgency I hadn't seen before. Had Su been right? Was he about to abandon us? Agitated, I made my way over. "Would you like some help?"

"Oh, no, no, I am fine." His calm tone quickly reassured me he wasn't about to ride off in secret. "Just preparing. I had to occupy myself somehow while you both sleep the day away!" He winked. "Ready for the forest, Belushka?"

"The forest?"

"Of course."

"Su thinks the road is the safer choice," I responded.

He raised his thin eyebrows. "Do you?"

I paused, and even though I agreed, I didn't like going against Su. "Well, I don't know if we'll get there in time if we take the road."

"Exactly! This is like war, you see. Sometimes the safest path is the one directly into danger."

"Did you fight in the war, like my father did?"

"Which one?"

"The big one, of course! Against the Germans. And then against the Reds."

"Yes. In my own way."

"Is that where you got your scar?" I pointed to a discolored line peeking out from the top of his shirt.

"Which one?" Vlad lifted his shirt, revealing a torso more

scarred than a butcher's chopping block. I stepped back.

"So, this must be why they call you the 'Deathless!'"

"I suppose so," Vlad said, lowering his shirt.

"How did you get them?"

"Each scar is a story, some more interesting than others. I will say this—never wake a sleeping bear!"

"You fought a bear?"

Neither confirming nor denying, Vlad lifted a corner of his mouth.

"And that one down the middle of your chest?" I asked. It ran from his chin to his navel, impossibly straight. Before he could respond, we noticed Su was making her way towards us.

She was yawning and smoothing out her messy hair. Without greeting her with so much as a "hello," Vlad announced, "The choice is yours: join us in the forest or take the road alone. Or turn back, of course. You are a guest on this journey."

Su stepped back, shocked at the violence in his voice. "I didn't realize I was a 'guest'!" she spat. She turned to me. "Do you just view me as someone riding along for a little bit of fun?"

At that moment I wanted to sink deep into the ground. "No, of course not, Su!" I stammered, trying to ease the tension. "It's just, like I told you before, I don't think we have enough time for the road."

"Make your choice, we are leaving for the forest in five minutes," Vlad added curtly. Su turned her back and walked away. He put down the blanket he was loading into the cart and rested a bony hand on my shoulder. Somehow, he sensed my trepidation, that gnawing fear inside me. His eyes softened. "There now, she'll come around. And don't despair, I am a man of the forest, remember?" I did, and I suppressed a shudder recalling the grisly scars he'd just shown me. "Don't let a man who carries dead bodies around for a living worry you."

"He seemed pretty adamant," I countered.

"If there is one thing I've learned, Belushka, it's that danger lurks everywhere. A well-travelled road guarantees nothing," — he grinned like a devil—"except boredom."

Boredom. That seemed like something far away, belonging to another life.

Su walked back over to us. I could tell she was still furious. "Okay, I will go. Not for you," she wagged a finger at Vlad, "but for her."

"Well, stop wasting time then and get in," he growled. He cracked the reins and the cart lurched towards the arch of curving tree branches that marked the threshold of the forest.

12

THE FOREST

As we entered, I began to shiver at the sudden drop in temperature. The air here felt heavy and damp, almost like fog. Though it was midmorning, the light struggled almost in vain to penetrate the tangled branches and heavy canopy, and it looked more like dusk.

"Listen to me, both of you," began Vlad. His voice was different, a bit like the tone he'd taken with us as we first rode out of the city, but this time even more colored with concern. "This forest is different from any other you have been in. There are all the dangers of any wild place—as well as dangers of another nature."

"What do you mean?" I asked.

"Words cannot do it justice, so I won't bother trying to explain. You will see for yourself. Forget what you believe is true, for it is true only in a small corner of existence." He drew a deep, pleased breath. "Ah, but it is the place for me!"

He seemed to speak to the forest itself when he called, "How I've missed you!"

Su and I watched in wonder as his hunched shoulders straightened and appeared to expand by several inches. It was as if he had been a wilting plant at last given water. And over the course of our travel, as we climbed hills, rolled through streams, and were jostled this way and that crossing root-gnarled paths,

Vlad only grew more chipper. "You two are terribly quiet," he teased. His voice sounded stronger and deeper than it did even earlier that morning. "Not scared, are you?"

Su scoffed. "What would I be scared of?"

"Ghosts, perhaps? Forest spirits, vampires?" Vlad replied. "Sprites, trolls or wicked dwarves?"

"Those aren't real," I replied.

"Oh, I see. You are much too worldly to fear such childish things, eh? But what about the Taotie's men?"

"I don't like the thought of them, that I can say," Su snorted.

"Ha! Soldiers—nothing but annoyances… there are much worse things to fear! Belushka, you like fairytales, don't you? I shall tell you one, to keep your mind off your worries."

"Um. All right," I was slightly taken aback that Vlad, one of Peking's most feared men, now wanted to while away the day with storytelling.

"Which one shall I regale you with? Choose your fancy!"

"The Snow Maiden?"

Vlad sighed with dramatic disappointment. "Overdone."

"The Frog Princess."

"Childish."

"The White Duck?"

Vlad raised a hand, covering his mouth as he pretended to yawn.

"How about Vasilisa and…" I began.

"Oh, what a bore! Give me something that won't put me to sleep."

I kept listing more tales, and Vlad kept acting as if reciting them would cause grave injuries to his honor. "I'm beginning to think you don't actually want to tell us a story."

"Not at all. When there is a worthy tale, then I will thrill you like never before."

"I really can't think of any others, we've gone through them all."

Vlad raised his eyebrows. "Think hard, Belushka. There is one more in that clever little head of yours."

I was getting annoyed reaching into the depths of my memory. At last it came to me, the story I liked least of all because it frightened me the most. "Koschei the Immortal?"

Vlad slapped the pony's reins. "Ah! Yes! Now, at long last, *there* is a proper story! I was worried we'd all be old and gray before you'd come to your senses. Koschei the Immortal, who was freed from his cell by Prince Ivan?"

"Yes, that story." I was not so keen on hearing it. With the dangerous journey we were on, I'd have preferred a more romantic tale, not one about a nasty old sorcerer.

"Even though his wife Princess Maryshka told Ivan not to open the door to the cell, he did and she even gave him water, which granted Koschei the strength to escape?"

"Yes. Ivan was quite foolish," I added.

"Or Koschei was quite cunning," Vlad retorted.

"I know why you chose this story," Su said. "Because you share a nickname."

"Well, that is no bad thing. A fascinating hero, isn't he?" Vlad winked. "Though I'm slightly more handsome, I should hope."

"No, no. Koschei is no hero." I was losing patience with Vlad's games. "He's an evil sorcerer who looks like a living corpse and brings great danger to innocent people. I'd say that makes him pretty much the villain."

"Ah, so, you only like lightness, Belushka? Sweet little stories with charming princes and friendly frogs? People do not like Koschei because he is like a pond reflecting the darker things in people's souls."

"But that doesn't make any sense. He didn't have a soul. Well, that's not exactly true," I corrected myself. "If I remember right, his soul just happened to be hidden inside a point of a needle hidden inside a goose egg, which was inside a rabbit, which was in a wooden chest buried deep under an oak tree on an island in the middle of the ocean."

"Ah, you know this story well."

"I've heard it a hundred times," I answered in a bored voice.

"An expert, are you? I bet you don't know that he was once a normal man, risking his life for his country. Just like your father. You see, Koschei was a great fighter in an ancient war. He was known across the land for his bravery and loyalty to all those with whom he raised his sword. But the day came when one of his fellow soldiers grew jealous of his nobility and skill. The soldier betrayed Koschei by telling the enemy where he slept that night. Poor Koschei, he awoke to ten sword points pricking his chest and he was thrown in a prison cell deep under the earth."

This tale did not begin as I'd heard it before.

"Rumors had reached enemy ears of Koschei's amazing feats, such as when he turned their cavalry's horses against them, put scores of their troopers to sleep and called in thunder and lightning to drive off the army. Many believed he was a wizard as no human could do such things. A diabolical sorcerer was summoned to extract Koschei's soul. He had become drained of all his spirit, and yet unable to die. The enemy could torture him for all eternity. Year upon year, Koschei languished in prison, forgotten by his friends. And eventually, forgotten by his enemies."

"But what happened to him, if he was trapped there for years and years?" I asked, finding myself unexpectedly drawn into the tale.

"Well, his captors neglected to maintain his chains and they rusted away. One day, they became so weak that Koschei broke free. But when he came up out of the earth into the light, he was no longer the muscular, handsome man so many ladies had once flocked to. Instead, he was emaciated and disfigured. He went home and the children he remembered were now stooped and balding. Nobody believed it was he and they chased him out of town. Riding his mare, he began haunting the dark corners of the world. Only she who had waited patiently for him all those years remained loyal. What a beauty. Her eyes, silver and daring. Her luxuriant coat, with its patch of white on her flank."

Sighing and gazing off into the distance, Vlad seemed to drift somewhere far in the past, but regained himself after a few moments. "And he searched for his missing soul. After years of searching, he found it at last. Never again would he be at the mercy of another."

"Where was his soul?" I demanded.

"That" — he gave me a wink — "is a story for another day."

13

THE BRIDGE

The deeper we ventured into the forest, the narrower and trickier the path became. Twice we had to get out and push the cart's wheels over stubborn roots and ruts. We found little to talk about, and as dusk came it summoned a great army of ominous shadows from the forest. I craved distraction like never before from the fears twisting and turning in my mind, including the thought I dared not speak aloud: *What if we're too late to save Papa?*

I needed something else to fill my head. Ever since we entered the forest, Su had been so quiet. Perhaps she needed some distraction, too. "Su, can you recite us a poem?"

"I guess so. What kind? Ancient, modern? About love, or about nature, or something from history?"

"Anything will do, really. Just one of your favorites."

She thought for a few moments. "All right. How about this?"

"Blue water… a clear moon…
In the moonlight the white herons are flying.
Listen! Do you hear the girls who gather water-chestnuts?
They are going home in the night, singing."

No one said anything for a spell, just drinking up the poem Su had delivered in her strong, clear voice. It was kind of electric, like the whole world became still and ripe and full, the way poetry can change everything in a moment. Then Vlad closed his eyes and recited:

"Perverse by nature, I'm addicted to fine lines
If my words don't yet startle people, I won't give up till I die."

Su's eyes went almost as wide as the cart's wheels. "*You* know Chinese poetry?"

"Bits and pieces. Du Fu is my favorite poet, but I see you have a fondness for Li Bai."

"Oh, yes, I used to be able to recite most of his poems by heart. My father was a scholar of history and poetry."

"Was he? I'd ask how such a man's daughter becomes a dishwasher, but I know these are times of cruel incongruence." A crafty look flashed on his face. "Li Bai and Du Fu were friends, were they not?"

"Yes, they had great respect for each other's work."

"Indeed, but they were from different worlds, Du Fu a drunken pauper and Li Bai a celebrated figure who had audiences with the emperor. Perhaps I prefer Du Fu because we have more in common. Neither of us are exactly upstanding citizens, are we? And we both like our 'fine lines.'" Vlad looked at her with his silver eyes. "You have the soul of a poet, Su. Yet do you know who you remind me of most? Mulan, so brave and so fierce."

Su gave him a cautious smile at the reference to the legendary ancient female warrior. Despite her misgivings, I could tell Su was warming to the rogue, though she would never admit it.

We rode on, falling into a comfortable silence, until the whoosh of rushing water steadily grew. Vlad pulled the reins, bringing the cart to a gentle stop.

"That must be the Dragon's Spine River," Su said. "I've heard my father speak about it. The locals say its shape was carved out when a dragon fell from the sky onto his back. The imprint created the riverbed. That is why it is so deep and jagged and twisty."

Vlad hopped out of the cart. "Well, let's take a look. I think our dear pony could use a break while we figure out how to cross."

As we strolled along the steep embankment, I was relieved to see a suspension bridge that would carry us over the river's dark, sprinting water. The bridge was narrow and rickety, though, not fit for a horse and certainly not a cart. Little more than a hodgepodge of lashed-together wooden boards, half of them rotten, the bridge looked wobbly even without the weight of anyone trying to cross it. Though the two ropes anchored on either bank that held up the bridge did appear thick and strong.

"The rest of the journey we will make on foot. I brought several sacks. We'll carry what we can on our backs. What we don't carry we can fetch later."

But before we could decide on what to bring, gunshots rang out.

———— ∞ ————

Angry bees. That's what they sounded like to me, evil metal bees flying at the speed of sound. I could see distant flashes of flame, which looked like little more than fireflies coming out for twilight. But when a bullet smashed into the side of the cart, exploding splinters every which way, I knew better.

Su grabbed my shoulder and tugged me down. "It must be the Taotie's soldiers!" she yelled.

"What do we do?" I shrieked.

Vlad was already moving, as calmly as if they were throwing eggs and not lethal lead slugs our way. "Get across the bridge. Try to keep the cart between you and the shooting."

"What about our supplies?"

"Forget it!" Su yelled, jumping out the side of the cart and pulling me with her. "Come on, Lucy, hurry!"

My brain told my legs to move, but nothing happened. I hunkered behind a front wheel of the cart and peeked back. The gunfire whizzed closer, heavier, and the dark forms of the soldiers began to materialize. There might have been eight of them jogging along, stopping to pop off a shot or two, then pushing forward again.

"Please, Lucy!" Su begged. "We have to run!"

But I couldn't. I was like a piece of petrified wood, something once alive that had become as inanimate as stone. I hadn't felt this way since my escape from Russia. Those memories layered onto my immediate fears, further petrifying me.

"What are you doing down there?" Vlad growled. His eyes met mine for a moment, and, seeing my terror, his irritation vanished. "Oh, very well. Get ready to scurry, my little squirrel!" He gave me a wink and, turning, even as the bullets clouded around him, he unhitched the cart from the horse. He whispered into its ear and gave it a slap on the rump. The creature bolted into the woods, well out of danger.

Vlad stood at the back of the cart and pushed on it with such effort that the veins in his face thickened like worms after a rainstorm. Slowly, creakily, the cart began rolling down the road toward the soldiers.

"What's he doing?" I said to Su, but by her dropped jaw I saw she was as confused as I was.

Vlad kept pushing, and I saw tongues of flame burst out from the front. Bullets tore at the cart as the soldiers concentrated their shooting on it. Now the cart was a rolling inferno and Vlad let out a cry as he gave a mighty shove. As if pulled by a team of racehorses, the cart hurtled at the soldiers. In a bewildered panic they jumped away to avoid being struck.

73

Red-faced, with patches of his shirt transparent from sweat, Vlad huffed his way back to us. "Perhaps now the path is clear enough for you, Belushka?" He gestured grandly towards the bridge like he was inviting me to a fancy banquet. My stone body came back to life and holding Su's hand, we ran to the bridge mouth.

She pushed me ahead. "You first!"

My stomach nothing but knots, I took my first step. The bridge swung and bucked like a drunken man. All I could think of was losing my footing and tipping over into the water rushing below.

I sensed Su following close behind me. "Just focus on your steps, Lucy," she said calmly. "One foot, then the other." The bridge seemed to stretch on forever. "I'm right behind you! Don't look back, don't look down — only forward! You're almost there!"

Step by step I went on, and at last I stood on the stable earth of the river's far shore. I spied a large rock nearby and dashed for it. Su was right on my heels, crouching for cover with me. From here we could run or hide in the woods. Except...

"Where's Vlad?" I cried, peering over the rock.

"He was right behind me. Oh, no!"

Just then, Vlad dashed onto the bridge. I could see the soldiers on the other side plainly, their green uniforms and even their faces, which were crimson and twisted in fury as they kept their rifles busy shooting at him. He was halfway across now. And then calamity struck.

With a loud crack Vlad fell, disappearing from sight.

I gasped. Had he been hit by a bullet?

No. I could just make him out flailing and struggling at the middle of the bridge. He'd stepped through one of the rotten wooden slats and despite yanking on his leg again and again, he couldn't free himself.

On the opposite bank, one man — he must have been the group

leader—screamed what sounded like an order to his troops.

"What's he yelling?" I asked Su.

She cocked an ear and frowned. "He's saying, 'Don't shoot, it's the man we want. Capture him.'"

Instantly the gunfire ceased and two men tossed away their rifles and ran for the bridge.

"We need to help him, Su!"

Not thinking about the danger or waiting for her reply, I jack-rabbited for the bridge.

"Lucy, come back!" I heard her scream behind me but I kept going. Funnily enough, unlike coming from the other side, this time I ran the bridge's wobbly length as if it were solid as a sidewalk, barreling along until I came up on Vlad. His leg was bleeding, caught in the broken slat.

"Go away, silly girl!" he rasped.

I ignored him and grabbed his arms, trying to pull him out. It was no use. And on the far side the two soldiers reached the bridge and started across. No time to think about that.... Perhaps if I widened the hole in the slat, Vlad could slide his leg through. I kicked at it, the wood so rotten chunks fell away into the river. But the soldiers were coming up fast now. They grinned when they saw all they were up against was an immobilized man and a frightened slip of a girl.

They were so close I could almost feel their breath.

Before I could think what to do, one reached out to grab me.

I heard quick footsteps behind me, someone launching into a leap—and then the soldier staggered backward as Su landed a flying kick to his chest. Facing the second soldier, she turned to me but kept her eyes on him, and said very calmly, "Hurry up and get Vlad out. I'll hold back this one."

Feverishly, I ripped out more rotten pieces from the slat. From the corner of my eye, I watched Su punch and kick the other soldier with incredible finesse. When the soldier tried to swing a wide punch at her, she ducked and then gave him a hard shove when he was off-balance. There was a shrill cry and a splash as he hit the water.

I knocked out the last piece of the slat and helped Vlad free his leg. I pulled him limping along the bridge. Su was coming up after me. But behind her, the first soldier she'd kicked was climbing to his feet and groping for a pistol on his belt.

"He's coming, Su, and he's got a gun!" I warned.

"Cut the bridge," panted Vlad.

"What?"

"The ropes—cut them!" He thrust his knife into my hand. I crouched and began cutting. Why did every part of this bridge have to be rotten through, except for these steel-hard ropes holding it up? I sawed away, now there were just a few strands to go...

"Watch out, Lucy!" shrieked Su as she came near us.

I looked up. The soldier raised his pistol and took aim at me. He was grinning evilly—until his eyes bulged, perplexed as the last strand of the rope gave way, the bridge shuddering and dropping out from under him.

As we ran off to safety, I couldn't say I felt terrible about that nasty soldier taking a cold swim.

14

THE SHADOWS

I could barely breathe as I helped Vlad, blood dripping from his gashed leg, hobble along.

"Do you need to rest?"

"I am not an invalid," he snapped. "Keep moving!"

Onward we stumbled, until the sound of the river faded and we found a quiet dell carpeted with soft grass. Peaceful, yet the soldiers' yells and the gunfire still echoed in my ears. "Are they gone?" I asked.

"There's no way they could cross the river without the bridge. We're safe — for now." Vlad plunked down. The strength the forest infused in him earlier seemed to have drained away. I sat next to Su, my spine against a tree. Suddenly, a wave of terror crashed over me. I thrust my hand into my coat pocket, sighing with relief. My doll Luba was still there, and so was the feather.

After a few minutes resting, Su looked as if inspiration had struck her and she broke the silence. "Ah, of course!"

"Huh?" I wondered what she could possibly be referring to.

"That must have been the water."

"The water what?" I asked.

"The wu hsing elements. You know, the five trials! Remember what the fortune teller told us?"

"Oh, you're right! So if we've done the Water Trial, now that leaves what?" I wondered. "Fire, wood, earth and... what was the last one?"

"Metal," Vlad said, blotting at the blood on his leg.

Su peered at his deep cut. "The soldiers could have shot you, but instead they tried to capture you – why?"

"I suppose they heard what a charming fellow I am." He was rather unconvincing, and pointedly turned back to poking at his wound. But I could tell that something was bothering him.

"You'll have to clean that soon, before infection sets in," Su observed.

"Don't worry about me, I've dealt with a few wounds in my time." As if reading her mind, he added, "I'm not quite at my best these days. Otherwise I would have gotten myself out of that little jam. All the same, a man must honor his debts, and I thank you both. Lucy, I never thought I would have a little squirrel help me like that. Or a girl with a head full of ancient poetry." He smiled weakly. "Where did you learn to fight like that?"

Su blushed at Vlad's compliment. "My father taught me."

"Ah, your father has taught you many good things. He has trained you as a warrior of the mind and the body. A wise man."

"He believes that with hard work and learning, all people can be great." Her voice quavered and I could see she held back tears. I knew she was worried about what would happen to her father if she didn't return. How would the sickly man survive without her?

"The greatest loss to civilization is the underestimation of character and ability," Vlad said. "I am glad your father understands that. Not many do."

Su nodded in thanks. "I underestimated you, I'm afraid. You are not as dreadful as you seem."

She said that with a straight face, which made me burst out laughing. "Oh, come on, Su! That is the worst compliment I've ever heard."

Vlad began chuckling, too. Actually laughing, not his typical sly snicker. "That's probably the nicest thing anyone has said to me in years! I put serious effort into being awful, so you must keep my glimmers of humanity quiet, lest my reputation suffer, and then all manner of trouble will find me."

"Our secret." I smiled.

He clambered to his feet, as if suddenly feeling awkward. "I ought to clean this."

"Vlad, you should not strain yourself," Su said. "Sit down, we'll go look for some water you can use."

"No, I am a grown man. There must be a stream nearby. I'll return shortly."

Maybe he needed some time on his own to recover from the earlier events. We watched him limp off. It was hard to believe this stooped figure in the distance was the same formidable man I'd met in the Badlands just a couple days ago.

I waited fitfully for him to come back. My nerves were still jangled from the affair at the bridge, and perhaps sensing that, Su began quietly reciting a poem:

"*Mournfully, mournfully rolls the Long River*
Saddened, ah saddened, the stranger's breast
The flowers as they fall his fate recall
As each flutters down in the earth to rest."

"What poem is that?" I asked. My Chinese was not good enough to understand all the archaic words, but I could pick up its melancholy tone.

"It is by a poet named Wei Cheng Ching. My mother taught it to me. It's one of the only things of hers I can always carry with me."

"This is what my mother gave me." Overcoming my

bashfulness, I took out Luba. It was the first time I had revealed her during the trip and it felt a little like announcing I was a kid, the last thing I wanted to admit even if I had to admit, deep down, I still was.

"Ah, that explains it. I saw her peeping out of your pocket and and it made me wonder. You never struck me as the type of girl who still plays with dolls. Why did you bring it along?"

"She's a link to my family, I suppose. My mother gave her to me before she died. I guess with my father missing, I wanted some sense of family being with me." I wasn't ready to tell Su the truth about the gems, or the plan for using them. Not yet. I just didn't have the courage.

Su shifted her legs. "Do you think of your mother a lot?"

"She died when I was so young, so it's hard to think of there being anyone but Papa from the very beginning, almost. But yes, I do think of her. Or I try to, anyway. But it's not easy. She only comes to me in flashes. Like the light coming through these trees. The memories create patterns, little flickers of light. I know she was there, but I can't remember seeing her. And to be honest, I can't even really see her face in my memory any longer." I'd never really put it into words like that. "What about you?"

"Less than I should. Sometimes the end of the day will come and I'll realize I haven't thought of her once. She was my blanket in the cold and yet, I forget to honor her because I am too selfish with my own thoughts."

"I think she'd understand, Su. I hear mothers are among the most understanding people on Earth. To be honest, I'm a bit jealous you had so much time with her. You knew her and she knew you. You loved the person; I feel I only love a shadow. But maybe missing a shadow is easier."

"Nothing is easy in life," Su sighed. "We can only endure our pain. 'Eat bitterness,' as we say in Chinese." She looked thoughtful. "Do you think they stay with us?"

"Like ghosts?" I paused for a moment, thinking. "I'd like to think not, but I just don't know. It is a bit different in my land. We believe people go to Heaven."

"So you don't think they are all around? Watching us?"

"Not really. But I guess maybe sometimes, if I'm in the right mood, and holding Luba tight, I can feel my mother's presence."

"Me, too." Su nodded. "Like now, I know she's near."

I could not say the same—my mother seemed even farther away once we entered this forest. And my father... he felt almost as far away now as my mother did. Was he alive or was he with her now? We both fell silent.

"Su?"

"Yes?"

"I'm scared." Once I uttered the words, I knew I had to be careful. Fears can take root, branching out under the surface, until without your even noticing, they have sprouted into mighty, immovable trees. We hugged each other tightly, relishing our shared heat.

15

THE FOX

"He's been gone for a long time. Do you think he got lost?"

The woods were quickly darkening, like a theater with its curtain coming down, all the footlights switched off. And like a theater shut after a performance, all was going quiet, the inhabitants scurrying for their places of safety before night overcame them. I wish we had such a place.

"I doubt it," said Su. "Remember, Vlad did say he was a man of the forest."

"But what if he fainted because he was so weak? Maybe he needs our help."

Su stood up, wiping the dirt and leaves from her jacket. "All right. If we are going to look for him, we'd better do it now before it gets too dark."

"Which way should we go?"

Su pointed north. "He started in this direction." I followed Su closely as she set out. Every now and again she would squat down and peer at the ground. Sometimes she even grazed her fingers across the dirt.

"What are you doing?"

"Looking for footprints."

"Have you seen any?"

"None. It's strange. You'd think with him dragging his foot it wouldn't be too hard finding his trail. But any trace of him seems to have vanished."

A chill blossomed in my belly. "Maybe he changed direction and you didn't notice?"

Su shrugged. "Perhaps, but it is getting too dark to see anything properly."

"Think we should stop?"

"I see a stream up there. You stay and keep an eye out. I'll go ahead."

"Are you sure that's a good idea?" I tried to chase the fear out of my voice but maybe the best I did was nudge it to the edges.

"I'll be right back, Lucy. I promise."

Su never made promises lightly, but as she set off, I still felt so alone, much like the first night when I was gathering sticks for the fire. I was worried about Vlad, and what it would mean for our quest if we lost our guide. I looked at the silhouettes of the forest, the darkened lines marking the trees bringing to mind a charcoal drawing.

I went to the stream for a drink. As I bent over, sipping, I gave a start at the reflection. An older woman with flowing long hair and sad eyes. I stared for a moment, transfixed by the sapphire and emerald tinted face just below the surface. Flowing gently in the direction of the current, her long blond hair resembled gorgeous swimming water snakes. In her hand she held a mother-of-pearl comb. Swept up in the beauty, I began reaching towards her.

A memory jolted me. "*Rusalka!*" I screamed, scrambling away from the water.

Papa had told me about the beautiful rusalka, spirits who lived in the rivers, tempted people into the water and drowned them. I ran, not stopping until the stream was out of sight. As I caught my breath, I laughed at myself. What made me hallucinate that? The stress of crossing the bridge? Hunger and fatigue? Whatever the cause, I felt that the forest was consuming me in its darkness. I heard a subtle rustling. "Su?" There was no reply. "Vlad? Is that you?" Silence. The rustling stalked nearer. My heart quickened. All my blood ran to my head. Should I run? But to where? I clamped my eyes shut, not wanting to see the horror, whatever it was, coming for me.

Leaves crunched. Whatever it was, it crept closer.

Something brushed my leg. I shrieked, waiting to be bitten, eaten, or carried off into the grim recesses of the forest.

But nothing happened. Uneasily I opened my eyes. Down at my feet pranced a furry animal with a beautiful reddish coat and a silky white belly. Large ears framed its eyes, which were like glowing green marbles, and it had a long, narrow, refined snout. Its bushy tail danced side to side. I knelt to get a closer look.

"Oh, you're a fox! Where did you come from?" She was rubbing herself against my legs again. I put out my hand, giggling as the fox gently licked my fingers. I began stroking her head and tummy. The luxuriant pelt felt like I was running my fingers through silk ribbons.

"Lucy! What are you doing?" I was so engrossed with this glorious creature, I didn't hear Su approaching. She was dashing towards me, her face twisted with shock. "Have you lost your mind?"

"It's fine, Su. I've made a new friend, that's all."

"You understand this is a wild animal, right?" Su said. "In China, foxes are not to be trusted. They're certainly not pets."

"This is just an adorable fellow traveler who wants some company." I gave her my best grin, hoping it might ease the anger out of Su's face.

"It's not a good idea. Foxes can trick you," she went on, "and even turn into a spirit or assume a different form."

"Oh, Su, don't be silly!"

"I am serious, Lucy." Her expression turned sheepish. "Even if it does sound a little bit silly."

I decided to change the subject. "Any signs of Vlad anywhere?"

"No. Nothing." She said that as if completely unsurprised. Then she grabbed my arm and pulled me towards the original grove of trees where we sat. "Come on!"

I looked back to see the fox sadly watching us go. "But... "

"Listen to me. We are in enough danger without the company of unpredictable critters."

It was dark now and we hurried back to the grove, where luckily, we found our sacks untouched. Exhausted from the day's twists and turns, we lay down and instantly slept.

I woke to the chirps of birds welcoming the dawn. There was no light yet and Su was still sleeping. At my feet huddled what looked like a dark lump. I couldn't make out what it was until the fox pattered over to my side. "Good morning." I stroked her long snout. "You found us, clever girl."

Su, awakened by the talking, stood up. "Lucy," she said, rubbing her eyes, "who are you talking to? Has Vlad come back?"

"No. Well, it's just..."

"What?"

"Our little friend returned."

Fully awake now, Su glared at the fox. "You mean, *your* little friend."

"Su, she was sleeping at your feet the whole night. Did anything bad happen?"

"No, but that does not mean anything. Foxes are sneaky. It was probably biding its time, working up some terrible trick."

"This little gal?! I think she just wants to travel with us — whether you like it or not."

"If *you* won't listen to me, I guess I'll have to try it another way." Glaring down at the fox, she raised an eyebrow and pointed her index finger. "You'd better not cause us any mischief, do you hear?"

The fox looked up, perking her ears and tilting her head from side to side, though her charms had no effect on Su, who turned to me, saying, "Don't claim I didn't warn you."

"Okay, okay. The moment she turns into a spirit or plays any tricks, I'll send her away!"

Su gestured towards a faint path through the grove. "Shall we?"

"What about Vlad? He might be limping along right now, looking for us. And then what will he do if he gets here and we're gone?"

The pitying look Su gave me, like I was a naïve child, rather annoyed me. "We have to keep moving, Lucy. For all we know, he could have abandoned us. You can't deny there was something strange going on back at the bridge. It was like he was not really scared by all that shooting. A little *too* confident. Maybe he secretly works for the Taotie. Or he wanted to get there first and nab the Taotie's riches. Or maybe he just wanted to get back to his casino in Peking. All I know is, he is not here now and if we are going to find your father, we can't afford to wait around for him. Remember, *you* were the one who said we didn't have enough time to take the road."

I nodded. She was right about needing to stay on the move. Somehow, though, I knew she was wrong about the rest. Vlad would never betray us.

The fox stayed close to my feet, clearly recognizing an ally, as we began walking. Soon my stomach growled and pleaded with me. I thought dismally of the bountiful food and drink we had to leave behind on the far side of the river, the hearty loaves of black Russian bread, the cheeses and raisins and other delights Vlad had packed. But all those things were gone, and there was no time to look for food now or even to stop to rest.

The fox trotted along, running through the bush alongside us. As we came to a clearing, she made a squeaking sound, then turned and bounded off. "Hey, wait!" I cried, racing after her.

"Lucy, don't go after it!" Su warned, pursuing me. Something sparkled ahead. It was a stream, its water rushing like quicksilver. The fox leaned over at the bank and lapped up the water. Even better, leaning over the stream was an apple tree, its limbs bursting with plump fruits nearly the size of cannonballs. Su had a huge grin on her face as we dashed forward, scooping the cool fresh water into our mouths and plucking apples, crunching into them with sheer delight.

"I think the fox was pretty helpful after all, don't you, Su?"

Su readied some kind of retort, but instead grabbed another apple and bit into it. I followed her example.

One thing did trouble me, however — the dimming of the sky. Passing through a clearing we watched billowy white clouds quickly expanding into great dark masses. "Looks like a storm is coming."

"Hmm, yes. We had better find some shelter," Su said.

"Let's go on a little farther," I suggested, though I hated to leave this oasis. "Maybe there's a cave or something."

After collecting as many apples as we could carry, we hurried off, searching in vain for adequate shelter. But the vegetation only grew denser and the ground became studded with jagged rocks and gnarled roots, hardly inviting.

"Think we should just go back to the stream?" I asked.

The fox began nipping at my heels. I tried to step forward, but the creature kept circling my ankles.

"Hey, you, stop it!"

The fox ignored my pleas, darting under my feet, trapping me in place. The high-pitched yip grew more feverish as she leaped in the air. It reminded me of oil in a sizzling-hot frying pan. Something had her all worked up.

"What is it? You can tell me, girl!"

She stopped jumping, raised her glowing eyes towards the sky and howled.

"Oh my goodness," Su began, awed.

"I know. I've never seen an animal in such a frenzy."

"No, not the fox." Su grabbed my arm and pointed upwards. "That!"

16

THE RIDDLES

Perched atop the forest canopy, on towering tree trunks, rested what looked like a wooden house.

"What is that?" I asked. "Why would there be a giant treehouse in the middle of the forest? It doesn't make sense."

The trees must have stood a quarter-mile high. There were no stairs or ladders. How could anyone go up or down?

"Well, *someone* must live there," Su said. "Should we find out who?"

"I'm not so sure. How would we even get up there? I, for one, would not be able to climb one of those trees. And if we did, who knows who or what we might find?

"We're lost. There is a storm coming. Anyway, my guess is that whoever lives there already knows we are here," Su said.

"Because of the fox?"

"No, because they are not like you and me."

"How do you mean?"

"They have the power of knowing."

"Come on, Su! Really... " But before I could finish my sentence, Su screamed, "There's something falling—watch out!"

Shielding our heads with our arms we skittered away. I heard the thud of an object crashing to the ground. We rushed over to investigate. "A bucket?" Three paper tubes peeked out from the top. A thick fibrous rope attached to the handle led back up all the way to the house. "What's in there?" I wondered.

"Traditional writing scrolls."

I noticed more objects at the bottom of the bucket. "Look, ink and a brush. Maybe there's a message we're supposed to respond to."

"Hmm. I think I know what this is about," Su said.

"Really? What?"

But she didn't answer, only reached into the bucket and picked out the first scroll. She unrolled it, read it and then did the same with the second and third scrolls.

"Well, what do they say?" So many times I wished I could read more Chinese.

"They're riddles."

"Riddles? Whoever is up there, is testing us?" I asked.

"So it appears."

"But why riddles?"

"Chinese believe riddles require great mental strength, that's why we call solving them 'shooting the literary tiger.' This person wants to test our intellects."

"Just what we need! A test!"

She ignored my sarcasm. "Let's see." Clearing her throat, Su began reading the riddle aloud so I could understand it: 'This lovely maiden prefers eating leaves to meat. She labors each day so that others may appear elegant. Who is she?'"

I thought about it. "Umm... I have no idea. Do you?"

"Give me a minute?" She closed her eyes. I always admired her power of focus. My brain was such a jumble of thoughts, like a stew made of vegetables and chocolates, many things that don't belong together. Su opened her eyes again, a small grin forming on her lips. "Pass me the brush and ink, would you?" Beneath the riddle she carefully wrote the character:

蠶

"What does that say?"

"The answer is simple if you think about it. That's the character for 'silkworm.' A silkworm only eats mulberry leaves and makes the thread that becomes silk, which is used as material for elegant clothing."

"You're right. You are so clever, Su!"

"Don't get too excited, we still have a couple more to go. And my guess is each one only gets harder." She picked the next scroll. "Yes. I think this one will prove more difficult."

"Don't keep me in suspense, what does it say?"

"'He devotes his life to looking after the house. His mate always follows the master when he goes out. A gentleman sees him and goes away. A villain sees him and turns away. Who is he?'"

"A dog?" I volunteered.

"I don't think so," Su said. "Why would a dog's mate follow the master and not the dog itself?" When I glanced down in frustration, she added, "Don't feel bad. I'm stumped too."

I put my fingers on my temple, trying to concentrate. Rain began pattering on my head. I shut my eyes and tried to filter out the noise of the rain and of my restless mind, taking hold of the clues, looking them over from every angle. "Looks after house... Mate goes with master... A villain sees him and it spells bad luck...."

Ah, could it be...? My eyes popped open. "Su! I've got it! A lock!"

After considering for a moment, Su nodded. "Well done, Lucy!" She dipped the brush in the ink and wrote:

鎖

"We are not half bad at riddles," I said. "Hey, where's the fox?" With all the concentration needed for "shooting the literary tiger," I'd lost sight of the literal fox. Though we both looked around, there was no sign of her.

"It *was* pretty strange the fox came along at all. She behaved more like a tame dog," said Su.

Foxes probably don't find riddles so exciting and I had a hunch she'd returned to the forest out of boredom. Ah well. "We're down to the last one now. What is it?"

She unrolled the scroll and read it out loud: "I can follow you for thousands of miles and not miss home. I do not fear cold or fire, I desire neither food nor drink. Who am I?"

This one proved the hardest of all, and I sat down on the soft mossy ground, barely able to think. Not knowing why, I reached for Luba in my pocket and placed her in my lap. Somehow, I sensed the answer was close to us. In what way? Physically close? Or a memory? Was it recent or distant?

Then I remembered the conversation I'd had with Su about our mothers—"I've got it! I've got it! I can't believe we missed this!"

"What? What's the answer?"

"A shadow! A shadow can follow you for thousands of miles and not miss home. It has no fear or desire. And it disappears at night."

"That must be it." Su brushed the final answer:

陰影

Then she rolled up the scroll and placed it carefully into the bucket with the other two. Instantly the bucket began a slow climb into the sky until shrinking into a barely visible dot above. A minute or two later, a loud whipping noise ripped through the air. We scattered as another object plummeted at us.

It thudded into the ground. This time, it was a rope ladder.

17

THE TREEHOUSE

The growing storm winds swung the ladder back and forth like a pendulum. I tried not to look down, but I couldn't resist the urge. Immediately I regretted it. The ground looked smaller and smaller, and so far away now. Only a fool would not be terrified. My palms turned raw from gripping the rope ladder so tightly.

I hoisted myself onto a large wooden porch. It was empty, and across the floor waited a door of rough-hewn wood into the house. Su, climbing below me, was as nimble as a monkey but still had a little distance to go. I didn't want to explore without her, so I stood at the railing, beholding the treetops spreading every direction below. With the cool evening mist, I felt like I was floating above the clouds, above the whole world. There was a sense of entering a mysterious, mystical realm. I gazed at the storm, which was now breaking down into a flurry of purple, gray and yellow tones. Then something skimming along the horizon seized my attention.

An airplane? No, it moved too slowly for that. It couldn't be a bird, not with that strange shape—and certainly not its massive dimensions. Nor did it have wings, yet still it soared majestically along the horizon, light glinting on its scales, until breaching a bank of clouds. I saw it vanish within, until there was only a tail. Could that possibly be what I thought it was?!

The next moment Su appeared and I managed, mostly, to

dismiss what I'd just witnessed in the sky. Like the Rusalka, the woman shimmering beneath the surface of the stream the other day, it must have been a hallucination. How else to explain it?

"Shall we go inside?" Su asked. I approached the door, which stood ajar, as if inviting us in, warm light spilling out from inside the house.

We knocked and called, "Hello?"

No answer. We tiptoed inside. The first thing I noticed was the odor, not offensive yet completely new to me, earthy and sharp. A tall wooden chest stood against the wall, containing perhaps a hundred drawers, each labeled with Chinese characters carved into the wood. Drying herbs were suspended from the ceiling. There was also a sprawling daybed scattered with plump cushions.

"What is this place?" I whispered.

She gestured to the jars of herbs lining the walls. "I think we are in a healer's home."

"But who would come all the way up here to get treated by a.... " I stopped short at the sound of rustling. Then came humming, and footsteps. From behind a carved wooden screen emerged a tall, slender figure. My breath caught at the exquisite emerald eyes and the most gorgeously sculpted face I'd ever seen. Her hair was a silky black, reaching below her waist. The woman's warm smile put me immediately at ease.

"Welcome, my clever friends. I am Kang. My apologies for not greeting you at the door, but you two are far quicker at climbing that ladder than any of my previous guests." She was grinding up a pungent, greenish-brown powder with a mortar and pestle, but gestured with a graceful motion of her head toward the daybed. "Please, sit, have a rest. I will prepare tea and snacks for you."

Su and I exchanged glances as she sauntered off. We sank into the luxurious cushions while the sounds of the mysterious lady preparing tea drifted to us from another room.

"Who is she?" I whispered. "Could she be dangerous?"

"She's obviously not that," Su retorted. Then she considered the matter a little more. "At least, I don't think so."

Before I could respond, the woman floated in with a tray of the most glorious delights: peanuts soaked in vinegar, steamed dumplings stuffed with wild mushrooms, fried bread, and many other savory delights. "You two are hungrier than newborn babes, which is plain to see. Please, enjoy."

I tried to be restrained at first, politely nibbling at the dumplings. But in moments, I was inhaling everything. We were both terribly hungry since losing our food in the river crossing. Eating hot food reminded me of being back in the city where I felt like the ground wasn't always coming out from under me — ironic, I guess, considering I was so high above the ground. The lady poured hot tea that slaked our terrible thirst. Only after I'd almost scarfed down all the snacks did I wonder if I shouldn't have accepted food from her. Something was strange about this woman — and not just that she lived in a giant treehouse. In an odd way she was familiar, though if I'd ever met her before, surely, I would never have forgotten someone so beautiful and enigmatic.

Taking a seat, Kang examined us as we lounged, sated, Su lying back on a cushion, hands folded over her satisfied belly. "There now, you must feel much better."

"Oh, very much. Thank you," I said. Well, it was too late now to worry about her putting something in the food — we'd eaten almost everything. I took another sip of the tea, which carried a subtle hint of berries. To be honest, it was one of the finest things I had ever tasted.

"Would your doll like some bread?" Kang handed over a

mantou, a steamed Chinese bun. I looked down to see Luba's head sticking out of my pocket.

I flushed in embarrassment, deciding the woman must have gone a little funny from living alone. "Oh, I think she'll be fine." I didn't want to be rude and tell her that dolls don't actually eat.

"Take this anyway, just in case you need to feed her. She is quite special, you know." I gave a confused nod, wondering how the healer would know it was a gift from my mother or that it was full of jewels.

"Uh, thank you." Not wanting to hurt her feelings, I took the bun and placed it in my other pocket, beside the Firebird feather.

"When I can, I always try to help troubled travelers."

"Who are you?" Su asked directly, staring straight into her eyes. The lady seemed unbothered, almost amused, by the direct question.

"A healer. But I think you have already guessed that. And, if I may be so bold, who might you be?"

"I'm Su and this is my friend Lucy."

"Ah. I don't get many visitors." She turned toward me. "Especially 'white ghosts' like you. And with impressive Chinese—how did you learn to speak so well?"

"Su is the best teacher in all of China," I gushed.

Kang gave a cryptic smile. There was something magnetic and alluring about her, yet she had a penetrating gaze that was so intense it shook my soul. In a funny way, it reminded me a little of Vlad. "Have you seen a Russian man passing by recently? With an injured leg?" I asked.

"I'm afraid not."

Su shot me an annoyed look at the mention of Vlad before turning to Kang. "Do you ask all your visitors riddles?"

"Did you enjoy them?" Kang replied, not answering the question.

"I am not sure if 'enjoy' is quite the word under the circumstances, but I did find them interesting," Su replied.

"I am glad. I love riddles myself. They keep my mind sharp, as I don't have much chance of conversation on my perch."

"Why *do* you live all the way up here?" Su asked.

"As I am sure you are well aware, the forest harbors many dangers. But few of them can reach me at this height."

"Why do you live in the forest at all?" Su probed. "I'm sure many valuable roots and medicinal plants are found here, but plenty of healers pick herbs in the forest yet still live in town."

"Towns and cities, they bring a whole different set of worries. I feel more in touch with the plants and animals right here." Again that brought to mind Vlad—both were souls of the forest. "May I ask what brings you so far from home?"

Kang listened closely as Su and I told her about our quest to rescue my father, sighing sympathetically when we finished. "What a journey you are taking! The forest has been in an uproar ever since this 'Taotie' character's arrival. Though I know of his terrible ways, I'm afraid I cannot be of much help in dealing with him. But the forest holds few mysteries for me and I will share what I believe might help you."

"We would be most grateful," Su said.

"You must first cross the Great Wall to reach the foot of the Phoenix Mountain where the warlord lives. On the far side of the mountain, that is."

"The Great Wall of China?" I clarified.

"Yes. It cuts through the forest. Unfortunately, it is very high and guarded by the warlord's soldiers."

That sounded perfectly terrifying to me, but it didn't much intimidate Su. For her, it was just another problem to solve. "How will we get past it?"

"With this." Reaching into her robe, Kang brought out a small silk pouch and handed it to Su. We both peeked at the dark green powder inside, sniffing at its musty tang.

"What is it?" I asked.

"It will put the guards to sleep. Now, if you keep following the path, you will cross a stream with an ancient stone bridge. Soon after, you will pass a tree that looks like two birds twined together. After that, you'll see the wall in the distance. Once it is night, get close—*quietly*, for the guards are alert—and dump this powder in the boiling water they use to make tea. After they drink, wait a few minutes, and you will find them sleeping more heavily than the dead. They are guarding a passageway through the wall, so once they're dealt with, there's no need to climb over."

"What if the powder doesn't work?" I asked.

She gave me a dimpled smile. "It works."

My eyes began feeling very heavy and I stretched out on my comfortable seat. "But how... will we... know?"

"You'll see for yourself in a moment. I put it in your tea."

18

THE OATH

It was the gentlest, warmest darkness I had ever woken from, and I didn't really want to leave. But something wet on my cheek started dragging me from the depths of my slumber. I slowly tugged open my eyes and stared into the green glow of the fox's eyes. The early morning sunlight dappled her soft reddish fur. "Hello, friend," I whispered. "I've missed you! We had quite the adventure while you were away."

Quizzically, the fox tilted her head—probably the most adorable thing I'd seen in my life—then wedged herself in my lap. At the sound of Su waking, she perked up her ears.

After glancing over, Su shook her groggy head in disbelief. "Oh, no! Not you again!"

"Reunited! Isn't that wonderful!" I exclaimed, rubbing under the fox's chin.

Su was still wiping the sleep from her eyes. "Where are we?"

"I have no idea. Remember, we both drank the tea."

"Well, I guess Kang made her point, the powder works—and then some," Su said. "What a strange place, a home high in the trees!" She looked thoughtful. "I suppose there is one good thing about getting out of there."

"What?"

"We just passed the second trial."

"Huh?"

"Where was the healer's house? And what was it made of?"

"A tree and—oh, of course! It was made of wood! So that means there are only three trials to go!"

"Which reminds me, we have the Great Wall to pass," Su said darkly. She reached into her pocket and took out the green silken pouch. "The last thing I remember was her handing me this."

"For the guards," I said, recalling something about that, and dreading the idea of having to get up close to the sort of men who back at the bridge looked down their rifles at us and then pulled the triggers. "But what about where we're supposed to go?"

"Wasn't there something about a bridge, and birds or trees?"

"I… I think so." My brain felt fuzzier than the fox's tail. "Well, we can just follow the path. It can't be too far, right? Besides, we have our guide right here." I smiled down at the fox. "She would never lead us astray."

"So long as a fox is *all* she is," Su replied. The way she glowered at the innocent, adorable creature almost made me laugh.

Though still sluggish from the tea, I knew we had to keep moving. It felt like my feet were two bowls of sticky pudding clinging to the ground as we plodded along. The trail was faint, a sign of how few travelers—human, at least—passed through the forest. The fox trotted next to me.

"Ah, there it is," I heard Su mutter. "Didn't Kang say something about a stone bridge?"

I looked ahead and saw a stone structure shaped like a half-moon over a stream, and more came back to me. Knowing we were on the right path lifted my spirits some—until I noticed, against the horizon and beyond a series of rolling hills, the contours of the Great Wall ahead. It looked like a dragon coiled on the hilly peaks ahead of us, the tall towers the spikes on its back.

Up, down, up, down, we trudged across the hills. Somehow, the Wall never seemed to get closer and the sun was sinking fast. How could the day have escaped us so quickly? When we spied a hut a short distance off the path, Su suggested we stop off inside before going on. It was a squat, one-roomed structure, constructed of dried mud and scavenged wood, with a thinly thatched roof begging for repair. The fox sat beside the doorway and curled up for a snooze. Before entering, I studied the Wall and could just make out tiny shapes patrolling along its parapets. Surely those were the Taotie's soldiers. I can't say that I regretted delaying our dance with them.

For a decade or more, it appeared, not a soul had set foot inside the hut. Dusty hoes and rusty tools leaned against the walls. A cushion in the corner was coated in inches of dust. Su picked up a small stone and used it to scrawl Chinese characters on the dirt floor. Even with this crude writing implement, I still admired the grace of her calligraphy. I leaned down to get a closer look in the dimness. "What are you writing?"

"It is a poem Du Fu wrote to his friend Li Bai. They were both famous poets, many years ago, in the Tang Dynasty."

"Oh, the poets you were talking about with Vlad?" At saying his name, I wondered where he might be now. Stumbling around injured? Making his way back to the casino? Or like Su warned, reporting our movements to the warlord? But no, I just couldn't believe that. Yet why did I trust him so easily? After all, he never denied being a gangster. Hardly a profession to inspire trust.

"Yes, the same ones," Su said, pulling me back from my thoughts.

"I remember him saying one was rich and the other was poor."

"Li Bai was known across the land and revered while he lived, but Du Fu was so poor that one of his children died from hunger. Despite their different fortunes, they respected each other immensely. They were both troublemakers in their own ways, which is why everyone likes them so much."

"Which one do you prefer?"

"Mostly Li Bai, but sometimes if I'm in the right mood, Du Fu speaks to me. Maybe, like friendships, one seems closer to someone at a particular moment of your life, though that can always change."

Su became pensive, and though she said no more I could read her thoughts plainly enough. "But we'll be friends forever, won't we?" I said, meaning to say it with more conviction than came out.

She looked alarmed at my question. "Of course, we will. But to do that, we must promise to try always to be understanding of one another. We must tolerate no secrets. Be there for each other always, and never tell lies." I nodded, feeling pangs of guilt for not coming clean about the jewels inside my doll. I couldn't explain why, but I knew that if I told her, it would complicate our journey somehow.

"Where I come from," I said, "we have blood-brothers and sisters. We prick our fingers and share our blood. It binds us together for life."

"In China, we do things a bit differently. We have oaths."

"Oaths?" I asked.

"Yes, it is a solemn promise we make together. To be always faithful friends to one another." She paused heavily. "We're about to go into certain danger. I think we can draw courage from an oath we make to one another. No matter what happens."

"Yes. I think we should do that, to make a promise that we will always be together in our hearts. Whatever happens," I said. "So, how does one of these oaths go?"

"I know a famous one from the countryside."

"That should do, right? How does it work?"

"Well, normally there is an animal sacrifice."

"You want to sacrifice our fox in an oath?"

"No!" Despite her serious manner in the last few minutes, Su couldn't help giggling now. "We don't need a sacrifice like that, I'm fairly sure. We do need an altar, though."

"How will we get that?"

"We'll make our own!" Su bounded up, grabbed the frayed brown cushion resting in the corner and stepped to the doorway, beating it against the wall, dust clouds billowing out, the motes dancing in the few rays of straggling sunlight. "Now, we'll need some stones." We scooped some from the floor, holding them tightly in our fists, then, following Su's example, I carefully arranged the stones in a circle around the cushion.

She dusted off her hands and studied our work. "Okay, Lucy, put your doll on the pillow."

"Why?" I protested, worried she somehow knew about the jewels.

"Because we need to be separate from our things if we want to touch each other's souls." Reluctantly I placed Luba onto the dusty pillow.

Su lifted her jade necklace, the one with the character for loyalty, over her head and set it beside the doll. "Now I will say the first verse, and you will repeat after me. Ready?"

"If you were riding in a coach
And I was wearing a peasant's coat
And one day we met in the road
You would get down and bow."

I repeated each verse using my best Chinese tones. Nodding, satisfied, and clearing her throat, Su continued.

"If you were carrying a teng..."

"What is a *teng?*" I interrupted.
"Shhh, Lucy. This is a sacred oath."
"I just want to know what I'm promising to do, that's all!"
"It's like an umbrella that a poor peddler might use when he is selling his wares."
"Okay, thanks. Go on."

"If you were carrying a teng," she said, looking over at me and smiling.
And I was riding a horse,
And one day we met in the road
I would get down before you.
I want to be your friend
Forever and ever without break or decay
When the hills are all flat
And the rivers are all dry,
When it lightnings and thunders in winter
When it rains and snows in summer.
When Heaven and Earth mingle
Not till then will I part from you."

The final verse lingered heavily in the air, and I thought about my friendship with Su, about how she had made me welcome after I first arrived in Peking, about the danger we would soon face together. As the spell of the oath faded, we looked at each other, wiping tears from our eyes. The hut was noticeably dimmer. When we stepped outside, it seemed that night had raced in. I wanted more light, but realized that if we were to approach and, somehow, cross the Great Wall, I'd better befriend the darkness.

19

The Tea

"Hey, where'd she go?" My fox had disappeared again.

"Foxes aren't adorable puppies, Lucy. It's just as well. We'll have enough trouble dealing with the guards."

"So, uh, what do we do if any soldiers find us?" Even expressing the thought almost made my knees knock together.

"How about, all things considered, we just avoid them?" We giggled, a welcome break from the rising tension. "But if they do capture us," Su went on, serious again, "there's no use fighting. They have guns. It's better to wait until the moment favors us — or at least until it's even."

"Su, there's something I want to say." A feeling of emotional fullness welled up in me. "Thank you for being here. I couldn't do this — any of this — without you."

"You don't need to say it, Lucy. Especially after we took our oath. It is stronger than anything we can say now." And without another word she rose to her feet, ready to get down to business.

We began picking our way toward the Great Wall. I wished this were spring or summer, not only because I could feel the temperature dropping, but because the crunchy leaves and dried twigs underfoot seemed to make such a racket when we stepped on them. You never realize how much noise you make until your life depends on making none. Slipping from tree to tree, always keeping watch for the soldiers who I knew were perilously close, we stole our way along. Soon a tiny point of light kindled ahead. It must have been a lantern or fire some of the soldiers were using. Now it was our beacon guiding us forward – into the teeth of danger.

We reached the Wall and clung alongside, creeping. I heard humming of a folk tune. Was Su really making a noise like that so carelessly? No, of course not – it was coming from a guard above. Su put a finger to her lips and we carried on, choosing our steps even more carefully.

So I really don't know how I scuffed against that loose rock.

It rolled away, not making a huge sound but enough for the soldier above to instantly stop humming. He scanned for the source of the noise. My hands gripped the wall, not made of stone or brick, but of earth that had been rammed together to a hardness of concrete.

All at once I understood. This would be the Earth Trial.

To my relief, the soldier turned away and resumed his tune, I suppose dismissing the noise as from an animal, and we went on, striving now to be even quieter. We approached a gateway piercing the wall and saw a fire with two soldiers huddled around it, holding their hands close to the flames. A teapot hung on a metal frame, the flames licking its iron bottom – the very pot we were to sprinkle our herbs into, I realized. We stalked closer, clinging to the shadows, waiting for some opening to make our move while the two men noisily slurped their tea.

"We need to draw them away somehow," Su whispered. "Even if it's just for a moment."

My mind was swirling and heart beating way too fast. Forcing myself to draw deep breaths, I calmed down enough to envision a plan. "How about we make some noise? Somewhere over there." I pointed to the other side of the guards. "Maybe they'll both go and investigate."

"But that would mean whoever makes the noise is stuck on this side of the wall," Su pointed out.

"True." I took another deep breath. "Okay, same plan, but once the guards go over to check out the noise, I'll run up and put the herbs in the teapot."

"You will?" Somehow, I was a little hurt at Su's surprise I'd volunteer for this task. "No, it's too dangerous," she added. "I'll do it."

"I'm the smaller one of us, so it should be me."

I could see Su weighing it all. "I suppose you're right. If we are going to get any farther, we'll have to take some chances. I'll find a tree to climb before I make the noise. Then after they come over, I'll get past them and we'll go through together."

"Be careful, Su." I squeezed her hand.

"You, too." She turned and crawled off, the darkness instantly swallowing her. I hunkered in the shadows, and it seemed to take half the night until anything happened, though it must have been only about ten minutes. Then it came all at once: a loud crash a few hundred feet away, sounding like a large branch falling from a tree.

"What was that?" Grabbing their rifles, the two soldiers stood, but the older one said, "Just a branch falling or something." He set his gun back down and returned to toasting his hands by the fire.

Su couldn't have heard this conversation, so she had to wait to find out the first attempt hadn't worked. Eventually she must have figured it out, for there was another crash, much louder, and this time it provoked a different reaction. "Just a branch, huh?" said the younger soldier. "Come on, let's check it out."

My heart jumped — the plan was working. I readied the pouch of herbs. Except...

"No. You go have a look," said the older soldier. "I'll stay here—in case there's more trouble."

"Oh, stay beside the fire, huh?" said the younger soldier.

"One of the perks of age, son. Off you go."

The younger soldier grabbed his rifle and departed. The older remained where he was, watchful and clearly not about to wander off. When we had come up with the plan, I felt so confident it would work, that all the pieces would perform just as I wished, like puppets in a play. Unfortunately, life rarely comes together in such a nice, clean manner.

Some yelling carried from the forest. "I can't find anything," cried the younger soldier.

The older soldier stood up and took a few steps over, about to shout something back. He walked toward the forest, his back to me. This was my chance! I shot up and bounded for the fire.

"Keep looking," the older soldier yelled. He remained there, scanning the darkness. I tiptoed towards the fire and pulled off the teapot lid. I dumped in the herbs, then replaced the lid and spun to run back.

I saw the younger soldier approaching. In another moment there would be no way he could miss me. My frantic eyes searched for somewhere I could run to. Nowhere but a pile of crates covered by a tarp. I dropped to the ground, belly-crawled over and pulled the tarp over me.

"Anything?" the older soldier asked.

"Nope. Around here, I'm not sure I really want to find out what it could've been. But it wasn't those kids the Taotie is looking for, I'm sure of that."

"Want some tea?"

"You bet I do. There's winter in my bones."

Stuck listening to their chat, I tried not to breathe, afraid they would notice the tarp rustling.

"How long will we be out here on guard duty, anyway?"

"I hear we're going to invade soon. Imagine the loot we'll get our hands on!" enthused the other. "Just imagine... all the gold and everything we ever wanted to eat and... "

The two went silent. Had they noticed the tarp moving? Footsteps approached.

It felt like my heart was trying to force its way through my ribs.

The footsteps stopped a few inches away from me. I was numb with fright as slowly the tarp began to lift.

20

THE TAILS?

It all happened so quickly, I didn't even have a chance to think of trying to run. As the tarp was thrown to the ground, I heard silly laughter.

Su's.

"You thought I ·was a soldier?" Laughter still getting the better of her, she kept at it, for some reason finding the situation hilarious. "Don't worry, they won't be giving us any trouble." I came out from under the tarp and saw the two soldiers fast asleep, teacups resting in their hands and mouths wide open, ready to catch flies. "And look what I borrowed from the older one." Like a proud warrior returning from the battlefield with a prize, she held up a spyglass then tucked it into her bag.

"Good. We got pretty lucky here," I said. "Let's go while the luck is still with us."

"No," growled a voice behind. "Your luck's all run out."

We spun and beheld yet another soldier. His bald head shone in the moonlight, and he bore a pinched expression, and, more importantly, a gun in his hand.

I looked at Su, her body motionless yet her eyes darting. How could she be so calm, when I just wanted to crumple? The soldier grinned evilly at us. "There's going to be a great reward in this for me!"

"Reward for catching us? Why?" Su asked.

"Ach, not for you! This one." With his rifle barrel he indicated me. "You're that Russian big-nose's brat, right?"

"You mean my father?" I asked, my surging hope competing with terror at the gun leveled at my heart. "A tall man with blonde hair?"

"Yeah, that's the one. I guess you'll get to see your daddy soon. The Taotie said to bring you to his fort if we capture you. Now"—keeping his rifle pointed at us, he rooted around in a crate and pulled out a length of rope—"I can't have you running away so—*aaaaaa-ooooow!*"

Suddenly the soldier shrieked. There was a blur of movement and the fox had her jaws clenched around his ankle! And then I saw something so extraordinary, I was mesmerized.

"Lucy, come on! Run!" As if being yanked from a dream, I stumbled away and fell in with Su. We ran and ran, Su gripping my hand so we wouldn't become separated in the darkness. Unable to see, I bumped my head and arms against branches and I heard Su grunting in pain, too. *Ba-woom!* There was a shot from a rifle, then men yelling somewhere behind us.

"Keep going!" Su yelled breathlessly to me. "If we put enough distance between us, they'll never find us in the dark!"

She was right. After several minutes, the soldiers' voices grew faint. We hid, panting behind a boulder, and fought to get our breaths back. "Lucy, what's wrong with you? Why were you just standing around like you'd seen a ghost?"

"It was the strangest thing. When the fox attacked the soldier, I could have sworn it had nine tails."

Su was alarmed. "Nine tails—are you sure?"

"I can't say for certain. I mean, there was a lot going on, and a lot of tails. Maybe it was seven, maybe it was eight. Definitely it was way more than there should have been. Do you think—well, do you think the fox might be a special one?"

That disturbed look on Su's face only deepened. "Special? What do you mean by that?"

"I mean," I groped for the word, feeling so silly, but continued, "When you were off in the woods yesterday and I got thirsty and went over to the stream. There was something *in there*. A woman living in the water." The image of the Rusalka swam vividly back to me. "At first, I thought it was just a reflection, plus my imagination, I guess. But I don't think so now. And when you were climbing up the treehouse, I was waiting for you and... Well, when I looked out, I thought I saw something flying."

"Flying? You mean an airplane?"

"No." I was so scared of what Su might think. I didn't want her to laugh at me for letting my imagination run wild. "I can't really tell for sure, but I think it was a ... dragon." I paused, letting that sink in, but I couldn't read Su's reaction. "I guess what I'm trying to say is, do you think that woman I saw in the stream, and the fox back there are... well ... you know, not of this world?" I wanted to say 'magical', but somehow it seemed too impossible.

Ordinarily, words came to Su's call like well-trained hounds so that she never hesitated when expressing herself, something I envied. I couldn't do that in Russian and certainly not in Chinese. But this time was different. "I think...Well, it must be that, or maybe... " It took her several attempts like this until at last she gathered her words. "We have entered some other realm, I think."

"I'm glad you don't think I'm crazy!" I thought about what Vlad had told us when we first came to the forest: *Forget what you believe is true, for it is true only in a small corner of existence.* He was right. Things were different here, and what we knew to be true once had completely changed.

"I've had similar thoughts, too. I just didn't realize it until you brought it up," said Su. "And I guess I believed all along that the fox was a shapeshifter."

"I know this sounds strange, but why do you think there are foreign creatures here in China? Shouldn't they be *Chinese* magical creatures?"

"You're a foreigner and you live in China, don't you? Why not those creatures, too?"

Yes. Su really put her finger on it for me. In some ways, maybe that was why I was able to accept this magical world more easily than I expected. Already I had entered a new realm: China. My life had been turned upside down when I departed home without my father, so what was the added discovery that magic lurked in some corners of the world, too?

"As for our fox," Su continued, "in Chinese folklore, fox spirits are sometimes said to have nine tails. That's why I was so disturbed by what you told me. They are complicated creatures. They can be good omens, bring riches or good fortune to those they take a liking to. But if they dislike you or simply wish to create havoc..." Su left the rest unsaid.

"Well, let's hope *our* fox doesn't have some cunning trick up her sleeve."

"She helped us out, so if she was actually a fox spirit — and that's a big *if* — then I would say she's definitely one of the good ones." Su shivered. "Well, it's not like we are going to get answers out here in the cold." She looked around and pointed. "Over there — see that mound of rocks? I think it's a cave. Come on."

Somehow the cave entrance reminded me of a mouth which would greedily swallow us, yet even so, going in was preferable to being caught by the soldiers. We squeezed in and fumbled our way through the darkness with our hands. Only a slender moonbeam reached into the cave's depths. Exhausted, we flopped down.

Just then, I noticed that this cave was not empty but crammed with heaps of objects. I grabbed something and held it up to the moonlight: a dented metal bowl, hardly a great treasure. It looked like most of the piles held similar items. "What is all this junk?"

"It is not junk!" a gruff voice shot out from deeper in the cave.

I nearly jumped. The figure belonging to the voice stepped beside us. I'm not sure where he came from; he must have been lying down in the dark.

"And I was enjoying a nice nap. Well, if you're here, I suppose I should have a look at you."

A spark flew and in a couple moments, an oil lamp kindled brightly. The man began stoking a small fire. Su gripped my arm tightly. As the face became illuminated by the fire's light, I noted his rail-thin arms and legs accompanied an unusually rotund belly. His neck was so thin I was surprised it held up his oversized head. I was about to ask who he was and where we were, but the man reached into his bag and pulled out a bun, which he immediately stuffed into his mouth. As he chewed, the long single hair sprouting from a mole on his cheek jumped and danced. It must have been a foot long.

After finishing eating, he rested his hand on his distended belly. "Ah, much better. The world is a finer place with a full tummy. Now, I daresay, I have some unusual guests." His eyes scanned us. "I've never seen a big-nose up close before." He peered at me closely, as if inspecting each nostril. "Yes, it's true, so huge, like a mountain growing on your face."

"Hey!" I protested, covering what I always considered was a modest-sized nose. "That is not kind!"

The man smirked. "It is only an astute observation. I didn't realize big-noses would be so sensitive!"

I was tempted to mention the long mole hair, but I held my tongue on that subject. "Who are you?"

"Me?" He grinned. "Oh, just a very hungry man. Especially for things that are not mine." He licked his lips.

"Are you saying you're a thief?" Su asked.

"Hmm, well, I suppose some might say that. I think of it like taking a sip of water from a cool stream on a hot day. A necessity. You can't judge a man harshly for that now, can you? Especially when the people you take from are not alive to care!"

Anger and disgust flashed on Su's face. "A grave-robber, then? Even worse."

With a mischievous grin the man leaned closer, putting his face right up to Su's, challenging her with an aggressive stare. His rancid breath made our eyes water. "I might ask why a fancy Chinese lady and some foreign girl are wandering around the forest." Su and I exchanged a glance, then she pushed her face into the man's, so the tips of their noses almost touched.

"Why do you care?" Su countered.

The man pulled back, intimidated by Su. "Simple. I've proven myself the helpful type in the past. Perhaps I'd like to help some more." He raised his eyebrows. "You need help, don't you?"

We looked at each other. Su and I did need help, but a grave-robber was not quite my idea of someone trustworthy. I squirmed uncomfortably and as I did, Luba shifted and her head peeped up from her pocket. The thief peered closer. His face brightened and eyes animated. "My, my, what do you have there?"

"A doll."

"Yes, I am not stupid, I can see that. Where is it from? It is quite a treasure, I can tell. One of a kind."

"What business is that of yours?" Su snapped. "It is not something you can have for 'helping' us."

I was taken aback by Su's tone. I'd never heard her so aggravated.

"My, jumping to conclusions, Princess! I was just going to ask

Big-Nose if she has fed it yet."

Su and I exchanged confused glances. In her treehouse the healer Kang had put the same bizarre question to me. "Why do people keep asking me that?" I asked the odd man.

"Oh, who else has asked you?"

"Once again," Su huffed, "none of your business!"

"Sheesh, you're both so sensitive! Never mind, perhaps you are right, none of my business." The grave-robber yawned, let out a loud fart, and patted his stomach. "There is only one reason people would be willing to risk treading through this forest, unless their mind has left them. I suppose you have some dealings with the Taotie, don't you?"

With only our eyes, Su and I held a conversation, discussing whether to reveal anything to this criminal. Sometimes if you really know someone, you don't need words to exchange opinions. Finally, with a few scrunchings of the face and dancing eyebrows, we decided it was worth the gamble to learn more. "We are looking for someone and need to find the Taotie's compound," I admitted.

"Well, it is not too hard to find. Getting in, now that's the problem. Guards everywhere, walls, traps, all that sort of stuff."

"There has to be some way," Su said.

"There is, but telling you comes at a price."

"What?" I asked.

"I haven't decided yet. Still interested?"

I didn't like the sound of this at all, but I focused on why we were here: to find Papa. What was one more risk? Reluctantly I nodded my agreement.

"Outside the fortress," began the robber, "there is a well. It looks abandoned, but if you go down it, you'll find tunnels that lead inside. Or so I hear."

"This well, how do we find it?" Su asked.

"I'd take you, but I'm heading the other way. Anyway, I don't wish to visit the valley that leads to Phoenix Mountain again. Never again."

"Why? What's wrong with the valley?"

"It is known as the Wasteland. Something lives in there that you do not wish to meet. You'll know you are in its territory when there are no animals in sight. Not even a single bird or cricket—they have too much sense to be there. That's when you know you're in its territory."

"What is it?" put Su.

"We locals dare not give it a name."

"Why not?" I asked.

"The people believe a name will make it belong here. It came only a few years ago, and they want it to go away, far away. The villagers nearby burn fires day and night to drive it off. Doesn't like flames, apparently."

"What does it look like?" I asked.

"Not sure. Nobody knows. They only know how it sounds."

"Well, how does it sound?" I pressed.

He snorted. "How would I know? I'm here, aren't I? But there are whispers about its whistle being more than just a noise." He stood, preparing to leave.

"Where are you going? You are not really leaving us in here by ourselves, are you?"

The grave-robber gave us an uninterested look. He got up and as he was disappearing into the darkness at the mouth of the cave, he turned with a smirk. "I have some graves to rob. It's been a pleasure." He took a few steps into the dark and was gone.

21

THE TRUTH

Though the robber's cave was a strange, cluttered place, we slept well there. Awakened by a blast of sunlight, I gazed from the cave mouth at the lush valley before us. Drops of gold, orange and yellow were scattered throughout the emerald-green forest, like spilled ink covering the foliage with an autumnal swath. Judging from the position of the sun, it seemed to be late morning.

Su came up beside me. Her face was smudged with dirt on her cheeks and forehead, her jacket now filthy and torn at the elbow.

"How beautiful," I said. "I can't believe anyone would call this the Wasteland. It almost looks like something out of a fairytale."

"And like most fairytales, bad things are not far away. Especially with the mysterious creature roaming about."

"Maybe the grave-robber was mistaken."

"Perhaps." Su looked toward the horizon. "Where you see beauty, all I can see is Phoenix Mountain." She lifted her arm, pointing to the distant, snow-covered peak. "And that's even if we get there." She pointed into the nearer distance and I saw two figures positioned atop a knoll. Soldiers hunting for us. "We'll have to wait a little bit. If we go now, I think they'll spot us."

"So, why do you think the grave-robber told us about the tunnels into the fortress?" I asked.

She paused, her face showing a faraway expression. "We can

never guess the motives of such people. Maybe he wanted to rob us, but realized we had nothing of value to him. Or maybe he sincerely wished to help. Probably we'll never know. I can only hope his advice is good. I'm just surprised he didn't tell us what we must trade in return."

"Do you think that creature he warned us about actually exists?" Something also tugged at my memories when I said that, but I couldn't pull the thread long enough to figure out why.

"Two days ago, I'd have laughed at that question. Today, though..."

I'd hoped Su would reassure me that the grave-robber's words were nonsense, a bunch of lies to scare us from going farther. But Su merely said what I knew, deep down, was the inescapable truth: the forest held many mysteries and occult powers, and we were at its mercy. Then her attention snapped away.

"Look! The soldiers are turning. It's our chance, while they're not looking. That's where we'll go." She indicated a section of the ridge, which would hide us well from the soldiers' prying eyes. But a wide, open expanse stood between us and safety. My muscles began aching at their involuntary tensing.

"We'll get through this together," Su assured me, sensing my fear. "Just like everything else." Hearing that, my spirit soared. I could be brave because Su showed me how. I was so thankful to call her my friend.

We rose and took off at a sprint from the cave. "C'mon, Lucy, faster!" I tried to put more energy in my legs and I picked up speed. "Almost there!" Su yelled encouragingly. "Don't stop now!" The ridge was quickly approaching. We were going to make it!

A ditch opened before us. It stretched far each way, so it would take too long to get around. We would have to jump. Su, a few steps ahead of me, launched and barely slowed her run when she landed. I jumped—but as my foot hit the other side, I staggered forward and fell.

I looked up at the knoll. One of the soldiers was scanning the area with a telescope just like the one Su had taken from the man who drank our special tea.

Su had paused, her attention divided between me and the soldiers. "Get up, let's go!"

I scrambled to my feet and set off toward her. As I ran, I felt something drop at my feet. My hand shot to my coat pocket— Luba! I peered back and saw her lying in the dirt.

"Lucy, what are you doing?" she hissed as I turned back.

"I need my doll!"

Su was now chasing after me. "No! Get back here!"

From the corner of my eye I saw one of the soldiers peering through his telescope at the area. He was turning in a slow arc— he'd see me in a moment! But I wasn't about to leave Luba lying there. I sprinted with all my might, grabbed the doll's flimsy leg, and swung back. Su clutched my arm and we ran on together.

I glanced at the soldier ahead. He almost had us in view and my feet were beginning to drag. Su pulled me, sprinting so fast it felt as though she were dragging me like a kite string behind her, my feet practically skimming the ground. Reaching the base of the ridge, we clambered up its rocky path and slid down the opposite side.

We'd made it.

Su frowned like a devil. "What you did back there—that was so stupid. Did you see how close that soldier was to spotting us?"

"Yes, I know," I muttered, abashed. But then her anger at me only touched off a rising resentment of my own, all the more so because deep down, I knew she was right. But knowing what is right and doing it can be unrelated animals. "You know how important that doll is to me."

"It's only a thing, Lucy! You could have gotten us both killed for a *thing*."

"No. You're wrong." It felt like all the blood in my body suddenly doubled, my veins struggling to hold it all in. "She is not just a doll, you know."

"Yes, yes, I know that," she snapped.

Her impatient tone set me off, and I knew I was stumbling onto dangerous ground. But when I get mad, sometimes no matter how I grope for the reins, a beast wakes up inside me I can't keep hold of. "You don't understand, Su. You don't understand at all."

Su raised an eyebrow. "What does that mean?"

"There's something inside." There. Now I had crossed the point of no return.

"What are you talking about?"

"Never mind. Just leave it."

"No, I will *not* just leave it. You risked both our lives back there—I want to know why. We made an oath, remember? That means no secrets between us. So what's inside?"

"All right! There are jewels! My mother's jewelry. I sewed them inside its body. The money we get from selling this is for when Papa comes." I drew a deep breath, then spat out the words like they were poison. "And then he and I go to America."

At once I understood what a dreadful mistake I'd made not telling Su about the plan for America ages ago. All along I was so worried about hurting her feelings. I told myself I was sparing her pain, but as I saw the hurt in her eyes now, I knew that I had been lying to myself, avoiding an action, which took more courage than I had in me.

Her expression glazed, like she was blundering through some nonsensical dream. "You are leaving Peking?" Her eyes turned to swords. "I am risking my life to help you rescue your father…

and you plan to abandon me at the first chance?"

"Su," I pleaded, but she wasn't done with me yet.

"You should have just stayed with your good friend Vlad! Gone off with him! You two are thick as thieves, after all!"

I placed my hand on her shoulder. "Su, it is not that at all! It's just. Well, you see, it's just..."

She swatted my hand away as if it were some filthy insect. "Just what?"

"You *have* a home, Su. Papa and I, we don't. We need a country, a passport. A home of our own."

"How is America your home? You've never even been there! China is your home now! I can't believe you had the nerve to swear that oath with me, knowing full well you were lying! Shameless!" She started down the rocky path but only made it a few strides before spinning around, her messy black braids flying behind her like whips, her eyes glistening with gathering tears. "You know, Lucy, I wouldn't have minded that you wanted to go. It's just that you lied to me. When you have almost nothing in your life, trust is the greatest treasure in the world. More valuable than all of your jewels." Without another word she carried on down the path.

"Wait! Su!" Hot tears flowing down my face, I threw myself after her. She glanced back and upon spotting me, started fleeing even faster into a meadow lying ahead, bursting with wildflowers. "Su! Wait! Please come back," I croaked, red-hot coals in my throat from trying to keep up with her, but after another moment she vanished among the shrubs and tall grasses. I walked on, searching through the meadow, which slowly thinned out and gave way to forest.

My regrets weighed on me so much it felt like my feet were shod in cast-iron pots as I dragged myself along. I wish she could understand the situation differently. Or maybe I could have explained it better? It was not some secret plan I had to abandon her, but my family's only hope at belonging somewhere. I wanted her to come, too, of course. But I knew that would be impossible. What was the use mentioning an opportunity for me that for her could simply not be done?

No, I understood now, as if the rising wind roaring through this forest penetrated my skull and blew away my illusions. A friend who couldn't be trusted was not a friend at all.

I kept searching. The silence was engulfing, like putting my head underwater. I was so fixated on finding Su that I didn't notice how the sound of my own footsteps had grown so loud. Alarmed, I looked up and around me. Where had the lush trees gone? Now they were skeletal husks, spindly and shriveled, barely recognizable as once-living things. Even their sparse, powder-dry leaves were as gray as their trunks and limbs. The afternoon sun was reaching towards evening, making the forest appear even more grotesque.

"Su!" I screamed. The eerie silence slurped up my voice into nothingness.

When I'd left Peking in Vlad's wagon, I was one of three, the youngest, the least experienced and the most afraid, yet always I could look to Su and to Vlad to show the way. Now, no one. Rising gusts of wind caused the trees to sway like dancing skeletons and spatter crumbly, dusty leaves on me. A sudden, horrid noise then tore through the silence.

I had never heard anything like it, a combination of booming thunder and the squeal of a slaughtered animal. A noise so nauseating it made me scramble and dive behind the trunk of a fallen tree. Only then, from behind cover with my heart galloping, did I look for whatever unholy thing could make such a sound.

At first, I saw nothing and I wondered if somehow my brain, unsettled by fighting with Su, had been playing tricks. But then a couple hundred feet away I spotted movement in the branches of a tree. A pair of wings. And a pair of arms? Surely my mind was conjuring illusions. But that thing *was* there, I was sure of it, with ash-gray feathers sprouting from pallid arms and hairy, manlike legs dangling below the branch on which it perched.

Its back was still to me, but I could see the creature gnawing the carcass of an animal it had caught. It finished chewing a bone and tossed it away, and when the creature turned to grab another one, I caught a glimpse of its blood-caked face. It was like some grotesque imitation of a human. A sharp beak thrust out where a nose ought to be, just above a human's mouth. One look at its face and I understood that the grave-robber had been right: naming gave something more power, made it far worse. But I knew its name.

It was called *Solovei,* or Nightingale. It was the nightmare of Russian fairytales and devoured all in its path.

22

The Nightingale

Just stay quiet. Eventually the monster will go away.

That's what I told myself, but though I made no sound and did nothing to expose myself, still the Nightingale turned around. Somehow it must have sensed me. The mouth gaped open and out rushed a bloodcurdling whistle, shrill and deafening. The trees around me shivered, as if trying to hide from the vile noise.

The Nightingale looked this way and that. At least it hadn't spotted me yet. Then it tilted back its head, sniffing at the air. Its eyes fell in my general direction, and it screeched in exultation. My scent must have given me away. Rising to its full height, the Nightingale bounded from branch to branch, then leaped off the tree and took wing, its savage talons bared.

Beating its wings it circled above, searching below with piercing eyes. I searched behind me for a hiding place better than where I was. Nothing. Looking down the length of the tree trunk concealing me, I spied a fat, hollowed-out tree just beyond the end of it. It would have to do. I slithered and crawled along, wanting to race but knowing survival depended most on remaining unseen. When I came to the end of the fallen tree trunk, I looked around, saw the Nightingale searching in another direction, and I dashed over to the hollow tree and plunged through the opening.

Inside was a tight fit, like the embrace of an overeager relative, but I hardly minded, overjoyed to be somewhere snug and secret. From the sound of flapping wings, I knew the Nightingale was circling above, searching for me. Was the Nightingale one of the Five Element Trials? If I could figure that out, there might be a chance I'd get out of this tree alive.

I closed my eyes tightly and covered my ears, attempting to block the assault on my senses so I could concentrate. First, there was the river, which was Water. The treehouse, which was Wood. And then crossing the wall, that must been Earth. That left two: Metal and Fire.

Fire, fire. Yes, that must be it! I remembered the grave-robber mentioning the villagers burning fires day and night to keep this creature away. I felt a momentary relief at figuring this out, only to recall the rather unfortunate fact that I had no idea how to make fire. Something about rubbing sticks together, or was it rocks?

But maybe it wouldn't even come to that. Outside my tree there was silence again. Forcing myself to calm down and slow my rapid breathing, I listened. Nothing. Perhaps the creature had given up on me, its last meal enough to satisfy it. I wouldn't need to fight, after all. Simply wait long enough to be sure, slip out of my tree and steal away from this godforsaken place. Simple patience, not fire, would be my weapon.

Suddenly the stench of blood and decay burrowed up my nostrils as a shadow crossed the opening of the tree. A face appeared, more wretched than it first looked, those awful eyes burning with furious hunger, which I now saw were human. Almost.

Opening its thin, bloodstained lips, the Nightingale howled and shoved its arm into the tree.

"Get away from me!" I shrieked. Mercifully, the opening was too narrow and the Nightingale's taloned hands clawed a finger's length short of me. With a horrific shriek it broke off and retreated from the opening, hissing and cursing in a voice that belonged neither to human nor animal.

Inside the tree hollow, there came scraping sounds from above. That confused me, and so did the flecks of bark raining down past the hollow's opening. Then, when understanding came, I went ice cold. Like some demonic beaver chewing through wood, the Nightingale was shredding the tree, enlarging the opening so it could enter. And I was trapped inside. All I could do was wait for it to happen. I watched the top edge of the opening break away, chunk after chunk.

Then a hand shot in, groping with filthy long fingers.

I pulled away but the Nightingale seized my arm and jerked me out of the opening. Tumbling to the ground, I stared up at the monster's cruel smile before his mouth opened to roar.

Yet not in the way I expected—not with delight at catching me, but with pain and fury.

And it let go of my arm.

Pushing my head out the hollow, I could scarcely believe what I saw.

Su was fighting the Nightingale.

Dodging ferocious swings of the monster's taloned hands, Su moved with grace and speed, replying to its strikes with thwacks and thrusts from a stout stick taller than herself. She'd found something she could use as a martial-arts staff. Though she landed blows that would have dropped a musclebound man, it wasn't anything human she fought, and the creature just seemed to shake off the hits.

But she wasn't really trying to stop the Nightingale. Only buy time for me. "Run, Lucy!" she yelled. "Get away!"

I clambered out of the tree and stood at the edge of the fight, frozen, feeling helpless. The Nightingale rushed Su, sweeping with his dreadful knife-hands. Su could fight the creature long enough to cover my escape, but what would happen to her?

The Nightingale swung its hand down from above, trying to catch her on the head. Su raised her staff and blocked, but in the split-second her weapon hung there, the Nightingale hopped forward and locked its jaws on the staff. Her weapon snapped in half and she jumped back before her foe could do anything more. With Su now unarmed, the Nightingale came at her.

She could only try to stay out of the reach of its terrible talons. And she was starting to falter, her dodges and rolls evading the Nightingale's attacks getting slower and slower. It pretended to swing at her face with one hand — but then pulled that hand back and swung with the other.

"Watch out!" I yelled, sensing some trick coming.

This time, Su wasn't fast enough. Her blood spurted as the talons raked her left shoulder and with the base of his fist the Nightingale hammered the top of her head. She staggered and fell, unconscious, like a snuffed-out lamp. The Nightingale grabbed her around the waist and its giant wings began flapping, surely to carry my friend off to whatever nasty lair it called home.

Then something strange happened within me. I should have been more terrified than ever, but I wasn't. I was angry. Once the Nightingale hurt Su, my fear vanished. I felt something more powerful than terror: loyalty to my friend.

Its great wings flapping, the Nightingale's feet lifted off the ground. "Let her go!" I bellowed, charging ahead and leaping onto the creature's back, seizing a leathery, feathery wing. I hadn't planned on it, but this was probably about the only vulnerable spot on the beast. The wing struggled in vain to stay in motion. The creature lurched sideways midair — and then we all three fell in a heap to the ground.

Su tumbled free of the Nightingale's grasp, out cold. I

clambered to my feet at the same moment the Nightingale did. It took a step toward me, its rage-smoldering eyes almost enough to crumple me. With a shaking hand I reached into my coat pocket, rummaging for some kind of weapon. There was nothing, of course—no knife, no gun. Only a dried-up crust of bun, Luba and the "Firebird" feather.

There was nothing I could do. Only try to make peace with my end. Wanting just a little bit of solace in those final moments, I drew out the feather. At the very least I would feel closer to Papa. Gripping it tight, I shut my eyes and waited for razor-sharp talons to rake me or to be smashed by the Nightingale's fists.

Nothing happened.

When I opened my eyes, the creature was staring at my hand. At the feather. It felt strangely warm in my hand. I thought I was just imagining it.

Until I looked down.

The feather was now an ember, glowing scarlet. And then it erupted into searing flame.

The Nightingale was hesitating now, no longer advancing on me. A scream of revulsion and fear escaped its pale pink lips.

"Get out of here or I'll burn you up!" I screamed, swinging the feather. Somehow its flame extended, so it was like I was wielding a great blazing sword. I pressed forward, poking with the tip, the Nightingale retreating, its wings starting to beat. Scowling and cursing me with one final appalling whistle, wounded and defeated, it leaped up and flapped weakly away into the night.

I lowered the feather and with my free hand shook Su. "Su, are you okay? Su?" I leaned down and could hear her labored breathing—at least she was still alive. She needed time and a safe place to recover. Still holding my blazing feather, I gathered some sticks, assembled a makeshift campfire and threw it on top. The wood burst into a column of flame. We were safe, at least for now.

Cradling Su's head in my lap, I wiped blood from her with my sleeve and whispered, "Everything will be all right. You'll see, my friend. You'll see."

23

THE FORTRESS

That dawn, the sun was shy, rousing itself slowly to waking. I did the best I could to clean Su's wounded shoulder. What should have been a simple process became tricky work, for my hands shook terribly, like tiny earthquakes pulsing through each finger. In some ways, sitting in the gentle morning light, I was more afraid than when we faced the Nightingale. I wondered if Su would forgive me or if things could ever be the same between us. Would our friendship endure as we had promised each other?

She began to stir. Peeling open her weary eyes, she gazed up at me, blinking, searching for focus. "Lucy," she whispered hoarsely, but was so weak she had to stop and take in a long breath before going on. "You ... you saved me!"

"And *you* came back for me! Why?"

"I had no choice." A small grin crossed her chapped lips. "With that big nose of yours, I knew you couldn't hide from that horrible thing."

With her teasing words, I knew our friendship would survive. "Su, I'm sorr—"

She interrupted me, lifting her hand weakly. "'*Forever and ever without break or decay...*'" she mumbled. This was her way of accepting my apology, reciting a line from our oath. She tried to sit up but winced in pain and gripped her shoulder. "*Ai ya*, that hurts!"

"Stay still. You shouldn't move yet."

She didn't even answer, nodding off instantly. I fought sleep long enough to see she was breathing normally, and then I gave in and shut my eyes, escaping at last from this nightmare world into my dreams.

It was early afternoon when I awoke, far later than I'd planned. I scrambled up. I saw the fire had gone out and was just about to wake Su when I noticed something among the ashes. There, its color brilliant against the gray soot, sat the Firebird feather, as clean and undamaged as the day I had found it on the train. I scooped it into my pocket, wondering how this was possible, then with a start my curiosity turned to worry at the idea of meeting the Nightingale again.

"Su, we'd better get out of here," I said, gently shaking her. "The Nightingale might have licked its wounds and could come back."

"I wish you were wrong and I could sleep another ten thousand years," she said, lifting herself up gingerly. "But we had better not chance it. Anyway, we have lost a lot of time here and should be moving on. The Taotie's fortress must be not too much farther."

"Who says you are going at all? Have you looked at yourself recently?"

She examined her cuts and scratches. "I've had better days."

"You can barely walk!"

"And you can barely tell east from west." Well, this was true. "Look, life does not give nuts to those without teeth."

"What do nuts have to do with anything? Have you lost your mind?"

"No, it's just a saying; life does not give challenges to those who do not have the ability to face them. Anyhow, if I left you now, halfway, I would have failed completely."

Su's jacket was threadbare, her pants ripped from the Nightingale's talons, her dirty face cut and bruised. Yet her eyes were as sharp and determined as a tigress's.

I had never been prouder of my friend.

Wincing, she managed to get herself up. Holding onto me with her good arm, Su hobbled along by my side. Back on our path, together.

———∽∾∾———

"Boiling egg drop soup. Except all the egg is gray."

"I was thinking something more like an upside-down ocean."

Ahead of us great clouds swirled about the sky like some chaotic mess, which, on reflection, I decided Su was right about: it did look like a swirling, terrifying soup. When an hour earlier we had emerged from the twisted forest, I thought I would rejoice from the open air and the afternoon sun shining down on us. What I found instead disturbed me.

The clouds looked heavy, like they were so swollen with moisture they had no business floating weightlessly up high. Something unholy was brewing above, and amidst it boiled a shadowy mountain. It seemed to scowl with malice, determined to protect the secrets which lay behind it.

"Well, at least we know which way to go," Su remarked. Neither of us finding more to say on the subject, we began our climb.

It was an arduous march, the path covered in loose stones which meant we had to crane our necks down to make sure we didn't lose our footing. Sweat rolled off me and I could barely catch a breath. Su didn't seem bothered, I guess due to all her martial arts training. After an hour's trekking — about the halfway point, we guessed — we decided to stop for a rest. Instantly I felt the freezing temperature. Our exertion had kept me warm, but now the sheen of sweat on my body seemed to encase me in ice. And I noticed snowflakes spotting Su's hair. She stuck out her tongue, giggling as she caught the flakes as they fell.

"You're laughing, at a time like this?"

"Well, in Chinese we have a proverb, 'Adding frost to snow,' meaning that something which was already bad, now is made worse."

"Oh, like being attacked by a half-bird, half-human monster only to walk into a snowstorm, all while we're on our way to the fortress of an evil warlord?"

Su gave an arch smile. "Exactly!"

Despite everything, I couldn't help grinning.

The snow fell heavier as we kept climbing. We could barely see in front of us. Su was starting to move more quickly, but she was still using me as a crutch. I was exhausted and losing feeling in my feet and my fingers were swollen and aching, but I knew that if we stopped, we'd succumb to the cold. So, onward we trudged.

For the whole of our ascent there was nothing to hear but howls of wind and our shuffling feet. Yet as we neared the summit, noises rose from the far side of the mountain: rumbling engines, muddled shouting, and a man's tinny voice yelling, "Form up, form up!" in Chinese, Russian, and another language which I guessed might be English.

Su reached the top before I did. "What do you see?" I asked, a few steps behind.

She didn't answer me, only stared down the other side of the mountain, shivering. It wasn't because of the cold.

I came up beside her. In the valley below spread a vast walled fortress, and at its center was a main building made of stone, a five-story Chinese-style castle. The middle of that was open, and treetops poked out at the top, like the castle had been built around a small plot of forest or a garden. Within the fortress grounds a huge mass of identically dressed men were running into position in long rows—it must have been thousands of soldiers. Eight behemoth tanks zipped along on their treads, lining up. A mighty war machine that could only bring suffering to untold numbers of people. And like some inhuman machine, the men just stood at attention, not making a sound, waiting for something to happen, or perhaps for someone to arrive. Honestly, I found their stiff silence more frightening than if they had all been shooting their guns.

Su peered at the disquieting scene through the spyglass she'd taken from the soldiers back at the Wall. "They must be getting ready to attack Peking," she said, her voice a mixture of anger and despair I'd never heard from her before. She handed me the telescope. I tried searching the faces of the soldiers. There were quite a few Westerners down there in the ranks. Where was Papa? For several minutes I scanned, scrutinizing anyone who didn't look Chinese, but I saw none was my father. And even if I did spot him down there, what might I do? Yell from the mountaintop, and wait for him to come to me? He would be held against his will by this giant army. Su and I had traveled so far, but gazing down at the scene below, I had no idea how I might help him.

"Who are they?" I pointed to three men walking across a battlement, a sort of wide stone platform on the top of the castle. I supposed it was designed for keeping watch on the area. As one, the men each lifted something shiny to their lips. Bright, crisp bugle notes suddenly blared. Below, the ranks of soldiers shifted in anticipation of something. Most of the men seemed excited, though others shifted apprehensively. Whatever they were waiting for, it was about to appear.

The notes played on in a fanfare, the sort of music I imagined would announce the arrival of a medieval king. After they completed their song, they lowered their instruments and stepped away from the battlement, out of sight.

A huge iron door set in the castle walls slowly ground open and out came something I didn't expect. Two soldiers gripping ropes, tugging hard on something I still couldn't see. It either was very heavy or very strong, for they had to drive their heels into the ground to heave out whatever was at the end of their ropes.

At last they got the unseen thing to move. Fighting against each step, a beautiful, light-colored horse was dragged forward. On its back rode a Chinese man in a military uniform which sparkled garishly from all the medals festooned across his tunic. He wore a helmet from which extended a pompous peacock's feather high above him.

The horse-wranglers pulled and pulled, the rider looking annoyed that he couldn't simply gallop along. But the horse had a storm in its soul, and clearly would have thrown the man if it could. Squinting as it came closer, I could just make out its silver color, with a patch of white on its left flank. "Su, the horse he's riding—does it make you think of anything?"

"Not really."

"The horse looks just like the one Vlad described when he told us the story of Koschei the Deathless. Remember, while we were rolling along in the cart? He must have mixed up his own real story with the fairy tale."

"You're right!" Su exclaimed. "Rescuing his horse was the whole reason he came along with us, wasn't it? I wonder what it means that it's actually here."

"Maybe it means he was telling the truth all along."

For a moment Su looked convinced. But only for a passing moment. "Or that from the start he was working against us. It wouldn't surprise me at all that a gangster could be useful to a warlord. They're all the same, really."

Heaving and shouting, the horse wranglers yanked the horse and rider towards a metal platform set up before the gathered soldiers. When they reached the platform, the rider pointed at a soldier in the front ranks. Immediately he hurried forward and dropped to all fours beside the horse. Careful not to be thrown by the steed bucking beneath him, the rider dismounted, using the man's back as a stepstool, then climbed onto the platform. Crossing, he stooped a little from the weight of many necklaces and charms draped around his neck.

He was smaller than I expected, and skinnier. Somehow, that made the Taotie seem even more dangerous.

He raised a conical megaphone to his lips. "Today we will move out and attack Peking. Show no mercy. It is the first pearl in a great string of victories we shall achieve."

As he spoke, sunlight glinted strangely from his mouth, but I couldn't see why.

"There is no force out there that can stop me. I have all the latest, modern military machines. And I will channel other, older forms of power as well."

Strangely, he pointed to the horse that so objected to carrying him. "Fight well and you will be rewarded. Show mercy and you will face severe punishment. Make your souls iron. The assault begins in five hours!" The Taotie concluded his address to the roars of his army.

The soldiers wasted no time, breaking ranks and hurrying this way and that, filling trucks with supplies, pouring fuel into tanks and airplane engines, and loading their guns.

Su turned to me. In her eyes, I could see she was daunted by the scale of danger we faced, but also as determined as I was to act. "Five hours—we'd better hurry."

24

THE TUNNELS

Though the fortress remained a bustling hive of activity with the soldiers preparing for the attack, still we climbed down the mountainside as stealthily as we could, scurrying from boulder to boulder. Towards the bottom we hid behind a cluster of rocks and peeked, searching for a way to slip into the fortress undetected. A wall ringed the whole structure, built of some strange material.

"Is that made of—oh, that's horrible!" I couldn't even finish saying it, struggling to keep vomit from rising in my throat.

The fence was not made of wood or stone, but instead layer upon layer of bones. Human skulls lined the top. It stood maybe fifty feet or higher, and its solitary gate was defended by about fifty well-armed soldiers. This time, we wouldn't be spiking any tea with herbs and waltzing through. I tried not to think of the people whose bones had become the beams and posts of the wall and prayed my skeleton would never join theirs.

Su pointed to a small ramshackle stonework at the base of the hill. It was barely visible beneath the branches and leaves covering it. "The well, see, there it is. Just as the man in the cave said."

"The 'man in the cave'? Don't you mean the grave-robber?!"

"Well, if you insist on being specific. But really, what choice do we have?" she answered simply. "Do you see another way?"

Unfortunately, I had no counter to that, and we crept to the well, which was camouflaged by thick tree branches. Carefully we moved the branches aside, afraid of making a noise that would alert the soldiers. There was a narrow opening, barely big enough for us to fit through.

"Let's see what we are dealing with here." Su grabbed a pebble and let it go. We waited and waited and waited. At last there was a far-off *clink* and a tiny echo.

"I wish we could see better," I said, then remembered the Firebird feather. Taking it out, I held it over the well, waiting for the magical light to dispel the darkness.

But the darkness held on stubbornly, for the feather did nothing. I couldn't explain why it wasn't working, other than that the magic was all used up. Su hadn't seen the feather in action yesterday so she only gave me a funny look. "Um, we could also just use matches," she said, taking one from a pocket, striking it and then sticking her arm down the well while patting at the slimy surface.

"How does it look?"

"We're in luck. There are some footholds." She stood up, wiping her hands.

"Do they go all the way down?"

"I guess we'll find out. Who's going first?"

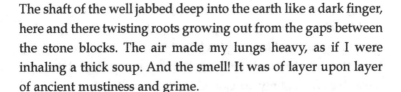

The shaft of the well jabbed deep into the earth like a dark finger, here and there twisting roots growing out from the gaps between the stone blocks. The air made my lungs heavy, as if I were inhaling a thick soup. And the smell! It was of layer upon layer of ancient mustiness and grime.

"You're getting there, Lucy!" came Su's yell from above. "Just don't look down."

Easier said than done, I thought, as I focused on staring straight ahead at the stone blocks. Only when I had to map out the next places for my feet to dig into the wall, or to step on a solid-seeming root jutting out, did I dare glance downward. This method seemed to work — at least it kept my fear to only a mildly nauseating level.

About halfway down, I hit an impasse. No obvious footholds in the surface, and the nearby root bounced under my testing step, so it would not support my weight. What to do? Finally I spied a tiny gap I might be able to wedge my foot into. I'd have to stretch my leg far and probably ask it to grow a few more inches, too. I took a deep breath and shot my foot over — yes! I made it in.

As I did, the branch dislodged a small stone block which fell away.

From the depths came squeaking and the churn of many wings. Rising fast.

"What is that?" Su shouted in a voice broken by fear and confusion.

I had no time to answer but I knew: bats!

They rose like a squealing, fluttering column, swarming and slapping me. Raw instinct brought my hands to protect my face and my stomach lurched at the sudden sensation of weightlessness. I'd lost my grip and I was plummeting!

Seconds felt like hours as I plunged, envisioning the bottom racing up to squash me. There was just enough daylight that I could make out a vague shape: a root! It was curved, growing out of the wall and looping back in. I bent my arm and shot my hand through the loop's opening. Darts of agony zipped through me as the crook of my arm jolted my fall to a stop.

That was close!

My legs swung wildly as I gasped in pain and at the shock

which had still not worn off. Honestly, I don't know how I hung on. Pure adrenaline, I suppose. Getting hold of myself, I scrambled into some footholds.

"Lucy, Lucy!" Su was screaming, her voice torn with panic.

"I'm all right!"

I caught my breath and looked below. The mossy floor of the well was only a short drop away, and I jumped down. "Made it!"

"Thank goodness! I'm on my way!"

I took advantage of the time to gather up my nerves. There was a single small opening, the start of the tunnel, I presumed. I waited for Su before exploring it. Within a matter of minutes, she was by my side. I looked at her in awe. "How did you get down so quickly?"

"I'm half monkey, didn't you know?"

"Su, don't even joke about that. After these last few days, nothing would surprise me."

She cocked her head. "Don't worry, I'm fully human, so far as I know. If I weren't, I doubt I'd be risking my life for the likes of you! I'd be out causing trouble somewhere and stealing fruit—I'd definitely not be in this smelly old well."

I agreed, the bottom of the well was not a place you'd want to hold a tea party. I lit a match and looked around, noticing a single tunnel leading out.

"Well, we made it this far," I said, trying to sneak more confidence into my voice than I truly felt. "And if Papa is somewhere on the other end of that tunnel, there's no other way for me."

Su squeezed my hand. "No other way for us, my friend. Come on."

We ventured into the chilly and damp tunnel, using our hands to navigate the labyrinthine darkness. Every few moments, we met a twist or a turn or another smaller tunnel feeding into ours.

Progressively the passage narrowed and lowered, so we went from walking to hunching to crouching to sometimes slithering. We kept silent, saving each precious breath of oxygen. At last we stumbled into a cavern that was the junction of two branching tunnels. Light leaked in through tiny shafts somewhere above, creating eerie shapes capering across the wall.

"I think we are here," Su said as she surveyed both directions. She and I peered down each tunnel but could sense nothing. There was only one way we would find out what awaited, and that was by going in and meeting it.

"So, which one do we choose?"

She bit her lip. "First of all, we are not going together. It is too dangerous that way. Better to separate now."

"What do you mean? How could you even say that?!"

"I'm looking for options."

"What kind of options?"

"The type of option you would need if some soldier were waiting for you at the end of a tunnel."

"I don't like it, Su. Remember what happened last time we split up? You know, meeting that friendly fellow, the Nightingale?"

"This is completely different. If there's trouble down here, we have no way to escape. Too easy for us both to get cornered if we stick together. If one of us is caught, the other can still do something. So you stay here and I'll see what is ahead."

"And leave me alone?" The thought of spending time in the cavern without her dismayed me. Whatever courage I had left in this quest of ours, it was flowing to me from Su.

"I will just see where it leads and turn back. Probably I will be standing here beside you again in no time."

"Well, what if you don't come back, then what? Shall I just die in this charming cavern?"

"We need to be practical, Lucy. You need to stay here, but if

I don't get back within twenty minutes, follow the other tunnel. But I'll return very soon. Just hold on, okay? I have always come back, haven't I?" She started down the left tunnel. I listened, straining my ears until her footsteps faded.

The ensuing silence brought back awful reminders of the Nightingale. I sat down on the cold cavern floor and took out my doll. Pressing her to my stomach, I could feel the hard contours of the jewels sewn into Luba's body. At first, I waited patiently, reciting poems in my head and humming folk tunes I'd learned when I was younger. But as time passed, the prettiest poems and most rousing tunes lost their power against my fear and worry... what on earth was taking Su so long?

Footsteps. Ah, there she was. Relief washed over me. I was just about to yell, "When did you turn into such a slow old lady?" when I spied a funny glint of light. I sank into a shadow and waited, my fears mounting. There it was again, another glint— the reflection of a lantern against a rifle barrel.

Soldiers!

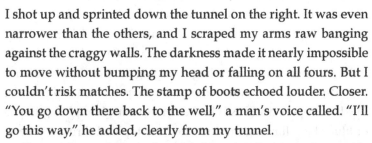

I shot up and sprinted down the tunnel on the right. It was even narrower than the others, and I scraped my arms raw banging against the craggy walls. The darkness made it nearly impossible to move without bumping my head or falling on all fours. But I couldn't risk matches. The stamp of boots echoed louder. Closer. "You go down there back to the well," a man's voice called. "I'll go this way," he added, clearly from my tunnel.

I moved as quietly as I could, knowing I was perhaps only ten paces ahead of the soldier trailing me. The tunnel narrowed even more, and the air was so thick with grit I wanted to cough it out of my lungs. And the soldier was closing on me but in this darkness I couldn't go any faster. Clearly these soldiers knew their way down here. As I went on, I felt an opening at the level of my head, a sort of shelf in the stone. I scrambled up to it and lay flat. More footsteps joined the first pair, and presently I heard both men speaking.

"Find anything?"

"Not yet."

"At least we got the Chinese girl."

My heart tumbled into my stomach.

"Yeah," said a second man. "And the Chinese one said the foreigner gave up yesterday and turned around. I don't know about you, but I'm not in the mood to bang my head down here in the tunnels."

Dear, dependable, quick-thinking Su! She tricked those soldiers to throw them off my scent! And, of course, she had been wise to insist we split up, otherwise we'd both have been captured. Which meant now everything was up to me. But what choice did I have if I wanted to save Papa – and now Su as well?

I recalled what Su told me about life not giving nuts to those without teeth. Were mine strong enough?

Moving on, still careful to make no sound as the tunnel would carry any noise to the two soldiers, I came to a staircase and climbed it. I stifled a cry of "ouch!" when I bumped my head on something hard and smooth and flat. With my hands I determined it was a ceiling. Groping in the dark with my fingertips, I felt the outline of a square-shaped hatch and pushed. The hatch opened and as I climbed more stairs, I caught a glimpse of blue sky. Climbing on, I reached the top and thrust my head into a world which, in my craziest dreams, I could never have imagined.

25

THE GARDEN

It was glorious, a feast of delights. Flowers, trees, and fountains, appearing in the whole spectrum of colors that can be found in the world. The beauty of the scene made me forget my fear as I gazed at fountains burbling, savored sweet fragrances of jasmine and other rich flowers enveloping me. Perhaps you could call it a Chinese version of the Garden of Eden. Ornate traditional buildings, gazebos and temples and pagodas, rose here and there, exquisitely constructed with black and gold lacquered wood.

After trekking through a haunted forest, and especially after crawling around in the depths of putrid earth, I had somehow stumbled into paradise.

Beyond the trees there were forbidding walls. I remembered how the fortress was laid out when I studied it from the mountaintop. I must have been in the central garden area, and those trees I had spotted were the ones I now walked among. The walls were of the fortress' inner castle. So, amid all this overpowering beauty and elegance, I now stood at the very heart of the Taotie's lair.

"Lucy!" suddenly a man's voice rasped behind me.

The voice was somehow familiar. Papa?! Spinning on my heels, I saw what appeared to be an enormous golden birdcage hanging close to the ground from one of the trees. In it was not a bird but an old man so emaciated, he looked more skeleton than human. Warily I took a couple steps closer and studied his face. His lightning-bolt scar. His icy blue eyes.

No. It couldn't be.

"Vlad?!"

The voice croaked in Russian, "Belushka, water, please." Now there was no doubt. But how could it be? The figure hunched in the cage was a wizened, dying man, not the dashing rogue I had been traveling with. "Over there." He gestured towards a nearby stone fountain. "Hurry."

I searched near the fountain for something to dunk in it, a cup or bucket, but found nothing, so I dipped in the corner of my coat then ran back. As if feeding milk to a kitten, I carefully reached through the bars, and dribbled the cool water between his cracked, parched lips and stained teeth.

"More, more!" he begged after finishing. This continued for several trips to the fountain. Each time, a little more color returned to Vlad's face. The wrinkles disappeared, his eyes rose from their sunken pits, his straggly hair thickened until eventually, and a shadow of the Vlad I knew looked back at me. His hair was gray and skin saggy as a ninety-year-old's, but his eyes again shone with their wicked spark.

"Vlad, what happened? Why are you here? And how are you...so old?"

He gave me one of his devilish grins. Not quite as dangerous as before, though getting closer. "Remember my nickname?"

How did I not realize this sooner? He chuckled as my face flooded with understanding. "Are you really Koschei the Deathless?!"

Placing his hand over his heart, he gave a courtly bow. "The one and only. Though these days, I often go by my middle name, Vladimir." He laughed, which unlike the boisterous laughter I knew, came out as an arid rattle. "I'm surprised it took you so long!"

"Well, I wasn't quite expecting a character from fairytales to actually exist!"

"A total lack of faith, Belushka. Stories all come from somewhere."

"What are you doing here, then? Why are you not lurking in a Russian forest?"

He smiled sadly, as if recalling good times long gone. "When first we entered the forest, I told you, did I not, you must learn to see and understand in new ways. And you have, though still you are a girl of your times. You must understand that mortals like you weren't the only ones driven out by war. My forests were occupied by soldiers and despite my reputation, I am not one to take on an entire army. I planned to wait in China until it was calm again, but I found I rather like it here."

I had so many questions. But one was most pressing. "Vlad, have you seen my father? Tall, with dark hair, blue eyes, and he stands very straight, like his spine was made of a steel bar."

"Ah, the colonel. Yes. Once. When they brought me in. Apparently, he caused them much trouble when the warlord's army attacked the train. After they brought him here, they tried to make him train the soldiers, who are mostly just peasants and run-of-the-mill cutthroats, after all, not real fighting men. He wouldn't cooperate and the petty little warlord had him whipped. A good man, your father just smiled the whole time and made jokes at the warlord's expense."

A rush of warmth and pride washed over me; that sounded exactly like something Papa would do. Vlad continued, "You see, the Taotie cannot truly lead anyone. That is why he has captured your father. Even from a distance, I could see he is a natural leader, a man who can hatch a daring plan, and then inspire his troops to shimmy around bullets to carry it out."

Yes, that was my dear Papa, all right.

Vlad lifted his wizened hands and sighed, no doubt recalling how only days ago they were clever and strong. "Now you tell me something, Lucy. My mare, Dusha, have you seen her?"

I related what Su and I had witnessed from our mountain perch, savoring the laughter he croaked out when I told him about the horse trying to throw the Taotie.

"It sounds like your father and my Dusha hold much the same opinion of the warlord." He paused. "I thought I sensed her close," he said, sadness now replacing his joy of a moment ago. "Dusha needs me, and I need her. It is only so long we can be apart. We share a bond which bestows my power. I had to summon my horse to Peking from her hiding place, so I arranged for that train trip. The minute the warlord got her, he began siphoning her power away. She was the surest way to get to me. Ah, if I could merely touch Dusha, I would be my handsome self again."

"Handsome?" I teased, raising an eyebrow. Vlad shook his head, smiling.

"Ah, Belushka! I'm glad to see the journey has not dulled your impertinence." It took me a moment to remember that it was in fact the villainous sorcerer Koschei the Deathless I was mocking.

"Vlad, what happened in the forest? Where did you go?"

Like an embarrassed child's, his ancient eyes fell toward his feet. "Koschei the Deathless, king of the rogues and scoundrels, fell for the oldest trick in the book. As you remember, I went off to deal with my wound. In a grove of trees, there was my Dusha. I couldn't believe it, so I ran over. Too late did I see how she was tied up, with soldiers hiding behind a tree. They dropped a huge net on me and next thing I knew, I found myself a guest in this charming accommodation."

"I know he is superstitious, but why would the Taotie want you?"

"The same reason he captured all the others in this courtyard. To use as his weapons." He swept a frail arm toward dozens of similar golden cages like Vlad's, many hanging from trees.

"Are all of these—"

Vlad cut me off. "Yes. Spirits, mythical creatures, magical beings. We still exist. But more and more on the fringes, for that is where these modern times are pushing us. People believe more in politics and machines and money now, so they cannot see us as they once did."

"But why has the warlord captured you all?"

He sniffed. "He would have us, like your father, all serve him, whether as his warriors or his playthings. The stories humans tell about us might contend we exist only to torment you, but there is more to us than that. Far more. We have our loves, our attachments. And that is the warlord's power, to discover those vulnerabilities and exploit them. That loathsome worm understands the weaknesses of mortals and immortals alike. That is his only strength: how to prey on the bonds between others. There are some creatures here who are not famous for their kindness—and I am certainly one of them—but it is *that* man who is the most monstrous of them all. And that is why you received help along the way, or at least you met so little real trouble from my kind."

"Besides you, who else helped us?"

Raising an eyebrow he gestured toward the cages. "Among these prisoners maybe you will recognize someone. Have a look, though do not venture too close. I don't know which are friendly and which are hungry." He gave me that enigmatic smile of his, the one I could never be sure was sincere or not, and with some apprehension I walked off to view the other prisoners.

In the first cage past Vlad's squatted a creature whose appearance words did not seem designed to capture. On four legs, it had a huge, distended belly and a face that looked as if it was carved from bone and wrapped with a thin sheet of leathery, gnarled flesh. Teeth the size of axeheads bristled in its giant mouth. Its breathing was deep and labored, as if there were a dozen rocks stuck in its throat. I shuddered, but when it looked at me with its sad pale eyes, against all expectations I felt a twinge of sympathy.

"That is a taotie," Vlad called from his cage.

"Taotie? Like the warlord?"

"Yes. That greedy man stole even his own name. The taotie was his first captive, I've heard."

I walked on to the next cage, in which stood a tall woman with her back turned. When she heard me approach she spun around and I gasped. A long, beak-like snout grew out of her face and her eyes were large and black as opals. Her hands ended in claws and talons like an eagle's tipped her toes. A *kikimora*, I realized — a Russian house spirit who haunts or protects a home. Not eager to chat with her, I moved on and came to another cage. Its occupant looked familiar — though in a different guise, as a statue protecting temples. A *qilin*, I think it was called, sometimes known as a Chinese unicorn. This one was anything but stone, though, bursting with life as it tested the cage bars with its antlers. It reminded me of a deer and a bull and a dragon all mixed elegantly together.

I passed other cages, one holding a *vodyanoi*, which is a sort of Russian merman, and another creature with the body of a tiger and nine heads that were almost human, arguing with each other about whose turn it was to eat the lump of meat on the cell floor, and many other creatures I can scarcely describe. But when I saw the prisoner in the last cage, I nearly collapsed in shock.

"Kang!"

The beautiful healer was leaning against the bars of her cage. "My young friend, you made it!" she exclaimed. "I've been thinking about you ever since the Great Wall." Her voice thickened with worry. "But where is Su?" As I explained what had happened, her lovely green-glowing eyes dulled with despair. "I wish I could help," she said, gesturing sadly to the bars imprisoning her.

"But I don't understand. Why are *you* here, along with these creatures? I haven't seen any humans in these cages."

She chuckled. "That is one riddle you didn't solve." Wrinkling her face in concentration, something *strange* happened. Kang began to shrink. Not only that, but fur erupted from out of her skin and her face morphed, growing angular and long, as pointy ears popped out. The next moment I was staring down at a nine-tailed fox which gazed up at me, its eyes the same deep green as Kang's. The fox pranced around the cage, then I blinked and suddenly, Kang stood facing me again.

"You *are* a shapeshifter! It was you who saved us from that soldier by the Wall!"

"Yes. I tried to accompany you as long as I could."

"So all along, Su was right about you!"

"She is an astute young lady and not easily fooled." Glumly she added, "It is men I usually have the most power over. But it has not worked on the warlord yet."

At the mere mention of that man, the spell was broken. As much as I wanted to stay with Kang, I knew I had to face what I dreaded most. "I'd better go. Don't worry, Kang. I promise to come back and get you out."

"I believe you," she said as I walked off. It sounded like she really did, and that unsettled me. The last thing I wanted was to let a shapeshifter down!

I walked to Vlad's cage. "I've been mulling it over," he said, "and would hazard a guess that your father is in the warlord's keeping, probably in his chambers."

He squeezed his arm through the bar, holding out his hand for mine, and I took it. It had the texture of paper yet still I could sense his strength sleeping somewhere deep below the surface. He looked me hard in the eye. "Even metal can rust. Remember that."

26

THE CHAMBER

I searched the Garden for a portal leading to the interior of the castle. Walking to the edge, I found only grim stone walls without doors or windows. I came to a pavilion with a covered walkway, lavishly carved and painted, and followed it along until stopping at a magnificently carved door. It bore a design, but not one I could easily decipher. It appeared that in the center there was a frame in which someone had carved an image from the dark wood, but the various pieces were not joined up. Weird. Well, I had other matters in my head than critiquing the decorating choices around here, and I reached for the doorknob.

Instantly an iron claw shot out of the door and clamped on my wrist. A contraption had been triggered by my touch and it trapped my hand in place. Invisible gears ominously turned. I looked up in horror at a sawblade slowly descending along the plane of the door. It was going to chop through my arm!

Frantically I pulled and heaved, but I could not free my hand from the iron claw. I tugged again. All that did was allow the sawblade to descend closer. I pounded at the door, not knowing what else to do, and the incomplete picture pieces scattered in place.

So they *were* pieces of a "puzzle." Maybe they…? Well, I had to try. Frantically I slid the pieces around, trying to complete a picture. Here was an eye, here a nose. Was it an animal? I tried a combination. No, it didn't work. This was the most high-stakes jigsaw puzzle ever!

There was time for only one more try. What could it be?

I took a guess, jamming the pieces together as the unseen gears turned, each click bringing the sawblade closer and closer. I slipped in the last piece...

The jarring, grating sound of the gears grinding to a halt was the sweetest music I would ever hear in my life. The sawblade lifted back to its original position, and I turned the knob and walked through the doorway, leaving the image of the warlord's face on the door.

In keeping with the sumptuous style of the garden and the covered walkway, the chambers I entered were unsurprisingly fit for queens and kings. Richly painted columns rose to the high ceiling. Antique Chinese scroll-paintings hung on the walls. It was like a wonderful museum of antiques and treasures. It reminded me of a much fancier version of Su's house.

Stupefied by the beauty, I stumbled through the cavernous chambers. Everywhere there were piles of objects: antique furniture, paintings, objects finely wrought in silver and gold. Probably the warlord had stolen them all.

From the next room came tiny, muffled noises. I stiffened, my heart pounding like a drum. Pressing my back against the wall I carefully peered through the doorway, holding my breath. I half expected to see the warlord, half expected to see a small rodent. I exhaled in relief when I saw two familiar messy braids.

"Su!"

She was chained to a bar set into the wall but upon seeing me, lit up as if nothing in the world could trouble her. "Lucy! I knew you'd come!"

"Are you all right?" She was dirty but seemed unhurt. I yanked on the chain, but it wouldn't give.

"It's no use, Lucy. Don't bother," she said, lifting the chains in frustration. "Only a key will spring me out of here."

I sat down next to her on the polished wooden floor and gently grasped her arm. "Tell me what happened!"

"The soldiers were waiting." I could hear shame in her voice when she added, "I tried fighting them but it was no use."

"Su, there was nothing you could do. It was an ambush."

"But..."

I stopped her with a finger thrust into the air. It was not the time to second-guess our choices. We had to stay focused on the future, on staying alive and finding Papa. "Do you know where the key is?"

She shook her head. I would have to find it. Before I went searching, though, I filled her in on what happened in the tunnels. Her eyes bulged when I told of my discoveries in the Garden. "I'm sorry for those creatures but right now we must do all we can for ourselves. Hurry and find the key! Before the Taotie or soldiers come back. Just get me out and we'll go and find your father together!" I nodded, feeling the weight of those depending on me growing heavier by the moment.

"All right, but I will be back," I promised. "Soon."

I stepped into a small hallway with two doors. I cracked one open and looked down a long corridor. Soldiers were coming and going at the end, and I quickly shut the door. At the other door, I noticed an unusual radiance seeping out at the edges. Frightened yet also curious about that almost unreal light, I walked in.

From the ceiling hung a giant golden birdcage, and within it roared a great blazing fire. Or so I first thought. I stepped closer and froze, dumbfounded.

It was far more beautiful than anything I could ever have imagined. No words could capture its exquisiteness. It stood to my shoulder. Its silky feathers shone brighter than all the jewels of the world. Awestruck, I stumbled over, shading my eyes against its brilliant glow. The Firebird turned and stared back at me with its sad eyes like two red-gold sunsets.

"Hello," I said in Russian. "I was hoping to meet you. The stories don't do you justice—nothing so beautiful as you is meant to be caged. Don't worry, I'll figure out how to free you and then we can..."

"How courteous," spoke a voice behind me as something hard pressed into my back. "How courteous of you to accept my invitation. I just knew you would come to me, Lucy."

The voice was high-pitched and raspy, an odious concoction of sounds I'd heard once before. I didn't need to turn to know who had crept up on me. In my surprise and fear I could only stammer, "I... I... "

"No need to speak, fair one. Frankly, I'd rather prefer it if you didn't. I expect silence from all the pieces in my collection. Now step forward."

He was the one with the pistol, so I did exactly as he ordered. After seeing him from a distance, the up-close view did little to improve him. His embroidered red silken robes draped loosely over his slender frame, but his back was stooped, as if he were a much older man because countless amulets and charms fastened at his neck weighed down on him. But a flash of his honey-colored eyes would scorch your blood, as if you were bitten by a viper. His head was cleanly shaven, and high cheekbones framed his wide nose and bleeding, chapped lips. He wore an infuriatingly satisfied smirk, as if he had been waiting all along for me to come, and now his plan had been completed perfectly.

I gathered my wits and found my anger at this monster who had taken my father from me and caused untold suffering to so many others. "I am not part of your collection!" I spat.

"You have a mouth on you! Lovely teeth, so white, like a

string of pearls. It would be a shame to see them replaced." He offered a vile grin, and the light reflecting from his mouth shot sparks of dread through me.

His teeth were made of metal.

"Ah, that rather quieted you." Keeping his pistol pointed at me, he moved to the edge of the chamber and took a large black key from a ring fixed to the wall. There it was! What I needed to get Su free of her chains! But now I had to free myself, too!

"It did take some courage for you to come all the way here, I must say. Maybe if you were not a girl, I would make you a soldier in my army."

"I would never fight for you!"

"Ah, don't be so sure. That is exactly what your father said."

"Where is he? Tell me!"

"Safely tucked away. He is going to be very important to my invasion of Peking."

I laughed. "You actually think my father will work for you? The emperor of Russia personally awarded him a medal for his gallantry. He'd never sink to serving a slimy toad like *you*."

"Oh, that's also what he said to me. You are undoubtedly his daughter! That's why he is sitting in a cell right now. But now that I have you, well, a father will do anything to keep his child safe. Anything."

Instantly I felt stupid and powerless, getting caught like this. Without it even dawning on me, ever since I departed Peking, I had been racing into a trap. I had delivered to the warlord precisely what he needed to coerce Papa into doing his bidding, no matter how disgraceful he would find it. He was right. Papa would never do anything that put his daughter, his Belushka, in jeopardy. It was just as Vlad said, the Taotie used the bonds between people, ordinarily such a source of joy and strength, to his own, wicked advantage.

"Yes, your father was most uncooperative, but now he will eat out of my hand like any other of my pets." He opened the Firebird's cage and waved me inside it with his pistol. "This will do for now, until I figure out a more suitable place for you. I am quite busy, so you can keep my darling company. He clucked his tongue affectionately at the bird. "She gets lonely sometimes." The cage door slammed shut.

27

THE CAGE

"Let me out!" Though I screamed, my voice got lost in that giant chamber. I rattled the cage bars in frustration, scaring the poor Firebird which flapped over to the far corner of the cage.

The warlord padded off. As he did, I spied the bizarre belt he wore: three dried monkey heads dangled from behind him, just as Su had said. He noticed my interest. "They watch my back — so try nothing silly."

Near the far end of the chamber stood a massive mahogany throne from which carved figures of taoties with gaping jaws stared ravenously. When the warlord sat down in it and flashed his steel smile at me, suddenly I understood: this was the Metal Trial I'd been waiting for. And it was not simply escaping the bars of my cage. It was to defeat the warlord himself. Deep in my bones, I knew this to be true.

I kicked the cage, pounded it with my shoulder, knowing it would be useless but unable to stop myself. "Let me out, let me out!"

"There now, don't get frustrated! It's your own fault — family is your weakness. I am helping you really, by releasing you from useless attachments. Fortunately I do not concern myself with such trivialities."

"Trivialities? What *did* happen to your family?"

"Ah, I broke their hearts."

"How?"

The Taotie gave me a sheepish look. "I stole everything they had. You see, I was born into rotten times. And then what does one do? Starve?" His sheepishness flickered away, clearing the way for wolfish pride to roar in. "No, one must become cruel or become a victim. Break all loyalties to others, and then spit them out like mucus in your throat! That is the only way to be truly free and strong. No one makes any claim on me, so my power is boundless! Otherwise, you will be weak, vulnerable, your fortunes bound up in the concerns of everyone else in your life. And why bother with others? Everyone is rotten, you see, deep in his or her heart. When no one is looking, most people will commit the most atrocious acts."

"Yes, but people try to be better, though, despite their nature."

I thought about what he said, and about all the evil things I'd seen in Russia. There are plenty of rotten people, maybe more than the good ones, but still I believed in kindness and loyalty — and thanks to Su, standing by me through great danger, I knew that I always would.

"Well, I suppose Taotie is just the right name for you. Though I guess the real one is locked up in a cage like this one. Why did you name yourself after it?"

"It was the first prize I ever captured, and I thought it a fitting title for myself." He beamed with grotesque self-regard. "The taotie has a major flaw: once it consumes something, it just stays in its stomach. So, I had a clever idea. We robbed a caravan moving huge quantities of gold bars and I got it to eat so much, that, well, it could no longer move. It had the honor of becoming the first in my collection."

"What about all those other ones?"

"Catching them took patience and cunning, both of which I have in great supply. I captured you with ease, after all." He shifted in his throne and sat up a little taller, clearly pleased with himself or, perhaps, simply trying to avoid sitting on a monkey head.

"And what about the Firebird? Why did you capture it?"

"Simple. It brings me luck. Everyone knows that. Though I don't truly need luck."

The warlord gestured to his vast army, visible through a window. "Behold all the strength I command! Cavalry, infantry! Machine guns! Tanks! Mortals like your father — and the creatures who will do my bidding. And do you know why? Because I have their loved ones! They are as weak as people! Even your friend Vlad. Hmm, I can see in your face that you think he won't? Ha! I only need to show what I'll do to that horse of his and he will be my slave. Now enough of this chattering, I have a city to invade."

He pulled a cord hanging from the ceiling and a distant bell clanged. In strode a man I'd hoped never to see again.

"Yes, your majesty?" asked Piggy Eyes. It was the Russian goon from the restaurant back in Peking, who had tried to make the owner pay 'protection money' until Su stood up to him. Seeing me, he smiled a smile even wider and more arrogant than the one on that day.

"What is the state of the army?" demanded the warlord.

"Ready to taste blood, Your Majesty. And I've just had a little chat with this one's father. He'll be our obedient dog now." He winked one of his gross eyes at me. "Nothing to say, Princess?"

"Only that back at that restaurant, I wish my friend had a chance to show you what she can do and send you crying for your mama," I spat.

Piggy Eyes darkened and looked like a volcano fit to burst. But before he could erupt, the warlord commanded, "I've changed my mind. Send word to the officers. I am moving the attack forward. We leave in one hour."

Piggy Eyes gave me one last irritated look before hurrying out to deliver the order.

"That Russian has his uses," said the warlord. "Some of the nastiest parts of the invasion plan were dreamed up by him, so I made him my captain."

But at that moment my thoughts were far from Captain Piggy Eyes — only an hour until the warlord launched the invasion of Peking! With all the forces he commanded, it didn't seem possible my adopted city could withstand the assault. And what could I do? I recalled Vlad's parting words, hoping they were true: "Even metal can rust."

My first task was to escape this cage. But as long as the warlord remained here, I was thwarted. How could I trick him into leaving? I scanned the chamber, looking among his treasure horde for some clue or inspiration. And I studied him. What were his weaknesses? My eyes passed over the charms hanging around his neck, the monkey heads dangling from his belt. He was greedy and he was superstitious. A plan began to form.

Even though it wouldn't understand, I gave the Firebird a wink, and then broke into the performance. My dramatic sobs echoed in the chamber and I freighted my voice with defeat. "Oh, I'm so hungry! I wish I hadn't forgotten my bag in the tunnel. There was some good food to eat in it, and maybe everything would be different now if only I had the magic charm the fox spirit gave me."

At those last words, the warlord's ears perked up. "Magic charm?"

"Oh, nothing." Warming to my playacting, I arranged my face into a picture of worry and regret.

"No, come now, you must tell me. A magical charm left in the tunnel? I shall have it!" He reached for his bell and rang it.

"Mr Taotie, sir, please, I'll tell you exactly where it is if you promise to let me out of this cage."

"Of course, fair one, certainly! After I have the charm. My captain will find it and bring it to me, and we'll know then if you are telling the truth and have earned a reward."

I heard Piggy Eyes' heavy boots tramping towards the chamber door. My escape depended on getting the warlord away from here. Out of nowhere, something Vlad told me at his casino echoed in my mind. *The wise gambler knows when to stop. The bold gambler knows when the only choice is to bet everything.*

It was time to take a chance.

"But Your Majesty," I added in a half-whisper. "Can you really *trust* him? The charm, it's very, very valuable."

"What does it do?" he asked, his eyes narrowing.

"The fox told me it makes anyone wearing it immune to gunfire."

"Hmm, bullets will be flying every which way as I'm conquering Peking," the Taotie mused, then he looked up as Piggy Eyes stepped through the doorway.

"Yes, Your Majesty?"

"Never mind. You may go. See that I'm not disturbed." Piggy Eyes glowered at me but then exited. The Taotie got to his feet. "In a few minutes I will return. If I do not hold the charm in my hands, well" — he looked toward the window — "we will discover if you can fly as well as the Firebird."

He walked out of the room, the monkey heads swinging behind him.

The warlord was right: we all have our weaknesses. And weapons come in all shapes and forms.

After his footsteps had disappeared down the hall, I got to work. "Now, let's see about this lock." Wriggling my hands through the bars, I awkwardly felt inside the keyhole. Yet no matter how much I pulled and twisted and poked, I was clearly not going to persuade it open. "How are we ever going to get out of here, my friend?"

"Oh! Maybe this!" I pulled out the Firebird feather and held it to the lock, concentrating hard. I imagined a gout of flame shooting out and cutting through the iron, releasing us. But just like at the well, the so-called enchanted feather didn't do a thing.

Hopping down to the cage floor beside me, the bird pecked at my lap. "Hey, what are you doing?" It was trying to get at something. Something about my clothing? "I don't understand. What are you trying to show me?"

The magical bird kept pecking.

"My dress? Oh, my coat pocket? This is all that's in here." When I reached inside and drew out Luba, the Firebird positively cooed. "Okay, so what about my doll?"

The bird was not done, now it pecked even more feverishly at my pocket.

"But there's nothing in here!"

It challenged me with those weird glittering eyes.

"All right, fine!" I really wasn't in the mood to be bullied by a magical bird, so I reached deep into my pocket, feeling something hard and crumbly at the bottom. "Nothing but this."

From my dress pocket I plucked a morsel of the stale steamed bread Kang had given me in her treehouse. "Crumbs, see?"

The Firebird squawked in delight and pecked at the doll. I let out a heavy sigh, because I sensed where this was going.

"Not you, too! Everyone wants me to feed this thing, but it's just a doll! Watch."

Feeling silly, I lifted the bread to Luba's lips. Of course nothing happened.

"I told you!" I turned back to the Firebird, raising my eyebrows. "See?"

The Firebird screeched, rattling the bars with its beak.

"Oh, what now?"

The mystical being I had once held in the utmost reverence, that I had struggled to envision when Papa told me tales of it, was starting to get on my nerves.

The bird grew even more agitated. It was staring at something. I squinted, trying to see where its keen eyes were set—the big black key hanging on a hook on the wall just behind the warlord's throne.

"Yes, I know! The key's over there and we're in here!" Again it motioned towards my doll. "There's nothing about her that will help us get out of here. I don't even know why I brought Luba with me. She's just something my mother gave me a long time ago."

What happened next was odd. Without warning, the Firebird stopped squawking. In that moment of calm, I looked into the porcelain face of my doll and considered how my mother, in her final hours, had given her to me, and I thought about how much I missed her. Scared and frustrated, I wanted solace, and I tried to summon her image now. But within my memories I found only fog.

Still I concentrated, feeling how much my mother loved Papa and me. And then something pushed through the fog, and I saw a smiling face, and knew it was hers.

Something wriggled in my hand.

When I looked down, I saw Luba chewing on the bread. She looked up at me with a huge grin, crumbs falling from its mouth.

I gasped. "My God! You are Vasilisa's doll!"

Why hadn't I realized this before? I recalled the stories Papa told me. This doll belonged to a girl named Vasilisa who was mistreated by her stepmother and sisters. They demanded she finish endless chores that were impossible for any human to accomplish. Before her mother died she gave Vasilisa a doll which the girl fed, just like it was truly a little child. It sprang to life and helped her complete all the chores, which infuriated her stepmother and stepsisters all the more.

As Luba nibbled, I held her lovingly in my lap, as if she were a tiny child. "When I put the black bread in my pocket with you, you ate it, right?" I asked her in Russian.

Guiltily, Luba looked away.

"Was it because you were trying to get strong enough to help me?"

Still chewing, she faced me and nodded.

"Can you help me now?"

Her blue eyes wide open and small lips still curled in an eager smile. I lifted Luba carefully up like a fine piece of crystal and pointed her towards the wall. "We need that key."

I brought the doll back to my lap.

"Do you think you can get it?"

For a long moment, she pondered the request, before biting her lip in determination and hopping out of my lap. She slipped through the cage bars, dropped, and bounded across the floor, pumping those tiny legs.

Upon reaching the wall, she stared up at the key. I would have to stand on tippy toes to reach it, and I was about seven times the height of Luba. She turned back to me seeking guidance. "Look for something to climb on!" I yelled.

From far off, voices carried into the room. The warlord barking angry orders. The reason for his anger didn't take much imagination. I was about to find out how the Taotie treated girls who tricked him.

"They're coming!" I called to the doll. "Oh please, hurry!"

After looking right and left, the doll scurried off to behind the warlord's throne. What was she doing back there? There was a faint squeaking noise—and the throne began to budge!

Somehow the tiny doll was pushing that heavy wooden throne, inching it toward the wall. But her progress slowed, and if Luba could breathe, right now she'd be gasping for air. "Come on, come on, you can do it!" I urged.

She looked up at me, nodded, and pushed again.

Nothing happened. The throne didn't budge an inch.

What could I do for Luba? Perhaps she needed more to eat? I salvaged for any last crumbs in my pocket. I found one and tossed it out near her feet. She had a nibble and instantly revived, scrambling up to the top edge of the throne and then jumping for the key. Again and again, she almost reached it, but never quite made it high enough. And with each jump she seemed more taxed and sluggish. "You can do it!" My encouragement put wings on the doll's feet, for she concentrated and launched off once more — and seized the keyring!

"Yes! I knew you'd come through! Now bring the key back down!" But no matter how she twisted and pulled, she just couldn't get the key off the ring.

A faint voice carried from outside the chamber. "She lied to me, the little brat!"

It sounded like he was down at the far end of the corridor, but still that meant he would step through that door before long.

"Try swinging on the ring, won't you? Like a trapeze artist," I called to her, which got me a blank look. Of course, a doll wouldn't have ever been to a circus! I motioned with my hands to illustrate, and immediately she understood. Swinging back and forth, tucking her legs on the downswing and pointing her toes on the way back up, she built momentum. The keyring grated as it began sliding against the hook.

"Tell the army to be ready, we go as soon as I deal with the girl!" The warlord was now screaming. He sounded much closer.

Still swinging back and forth, faster and faster, Luba threw all her strength forward and the keyring leaped off the hook and clattered on the floor. Propelled by the force, she hit the ground and rolled until coming to a stop. She didn't get up.

The key rested a few feet outside my cage. I wriggled my arm through the bar and reached for it. "No, no!" I wailed. It was close, but not close enough.

"Please!" I begged. "I know why you first came to me. Before my mama died, somehow, she sent you! Because she knew I'd need her but she couldn't be there for me! But I need help! Please, Luba! Get up! You can do it!"

Then, just as my last shred of hope was vanishing, a twitch from Luba. She lifted an arm. "Yes! Oh, please get up, hurry!" I cried. A leg wriggled, her head turned. Then she sat up. "Come on, come on!" Despite being so very weak, she found the strength to crawl across the floor toward the key. She came to it and with a supreme effort, began dragging it toward me. I prayed the warlord would stay away just a moment longer. I reached through the bars, but the doll was not yet close enough. She pulled the key more furiously and dropped to the floor, unmoving. Stretching my arm until it hurt, I reached out... Yes, I could just brush the keys...

But only with my fingertips. I was stretched to the limit, and it wasn't enough. I just couldn't pull the key closer.

My doll's eyes fluttered open. Screwing up her face with determination, she fought to her feet, dragged the keys a little closer, then collapsed. I reached out—and seized the key! "Got it!" I shouted with joy as I pushed the key towards the lock.

The chamber door swung open. In marched the warlord, trailed by seven soldiers. Seeing in an instant what was happening, he jabbed a finger at me. "Stop her!" he snapped. "Don't let her escape!"

I quickly inserted the key, turned the lock, and threw open

the cage door. "You're free!" I urged the Firebird as I leaped out.

"Grab the girl!" the Taotie commanded. "Quick, close the cage, before the bird gets away!"

Two soldiers rushed, trying to scoop me up. I darted away toward the door, screaming "Fly, you're free!" to the Firebird. But the creature wouldn't move. I was almost at the door when the Taotie blocked my path, and I stared into the black abyss of his pistol barrel.

"You, naughty girl, are simply too much trouble." He cocked his gun. "And your father doesn't need to know you're no longer with us." He pointed the gun at me.

A deafening blast ... a fiery flash of light.

28

The Battle

Intense heat washed over me. Light pushed through my clamped eyelids. With quaking fingers I reached for my chest, expecting to touch a grievous wound.

No blood. No pain. Only rapidly growing heat. I opened my eyes and turned to see the source—and gasped in wonder.

The Firebird, standing at the cage door, had ignited in flame. No longer a soft glow but a blinding wreath of fire. And what I'd thought was a gunshot was actually the creature, for again it trumpeted a deafening call.

With a burst of flame it flew out of the cage, trailing golden fire throughout the room as it circled overhead. It swooped at the Taotie but he dived for safety.

Again the Firebird circled and swooped. One soldier raised his rifle and aimed.

"Watch out!" I warned the Firebird. It shot a blazing plume at the soldier, which curled around his rifle and caused it to burst into flame. The soldiers stayed behind cover, shaking in terror. This was my chance.

"Thank you!" I yelled to the Firebird, snatched the key out of the cage's lock and dashed from the room.

"After her!" I heard the warlord scream. A few soldiers crawled out from their hiding place behind the warlord's throne and pursued me.

I bounded into the next room shouting, "Su! Su!" The soldiers were almost in grabbing range of me.

"Lucy!" She jumped to her feet.

With no time to free her, I tossed her the key and raced on through the open doorway into the long hallway. "Get out of here!" I yelled as I ran as fast as my legs could carry me. Running wild, as I wasn't sure where I was going. I rounded a bend. The warlord and his men were gaining on me. On and on I sprinted, down corridors, up flights of stairs, through giant rooms and tiny ones, the peculiar blended details of a medieval palace and a modern military base passing me by in a blur. All the time I searched for somewhere I could lose my dogged pursuers. But their boots kept clomping after me.

I spied an open doorway, sped through it, and found myself in a narrow spiral stairwell.

"We have her!" I heard the warlord crow behind me.

With no other choice, I raced up the stairs, following turn after turn as I climbed higher, the soldiers' voices and boots echoing behind. At the top I threw open the door and felt icy wind on my face. It was the battlement, the platform crowning the fortress where the buglers had played. I ran to the edge and looked over—nothing but a long, long drop to the hard ground below. And the Taotie and his men were now filing through the doorway, their guns drawn.

The Taotie's wrath-red face and shining steel teeth gave him a more demonic presence than any of the creatures I had met in the Garden. "Step away from there. Do not pretend you have any choice."

I did as he said.

"What were you thinking? That by letting the Firebird out, my plans would be foiled? Ha! It is an inconvenience, but hardly enough to stop me!"

So this was how it would end for me. To come so far, to endure such hardships, only for a greedy and dreadful man to win. Part of me wanted to weep, but the bigger, stronger part wasn't crushed yet, and I met his eyes with the most withering glare I could muster.

A soldier standing near the doorway looked suddenly alarmed. "Who's there?" he challenged, shouting down the stairwell from which came the faint sound of footsteps.

No response, only the continuing echo of the steps getting closer. "Your Majesty! Someone's coming! It's not one of ours!"

"Bolt that door!" the warlord commanded. The soldier slammed the heavy cast iron door shut and shot the bolt.

Bam! The door flew off its hinges. In the doorway appeared Vlad, still elderly but apparently having scraped up some strength—and then some.

He strode onto the battlements. At his feet, a russet streak blurred past him, closing on the nearest soldier. The man raised his rifle but it was as if he moved in slow-motion, the blur leaping at his chest and knocking him down. For a split-second at the point of impact I could just make out nine tails.

The fox's green eyes flashed at me, and there was a hint of a smile before she bounded on four legs at the next soldier. "Yow!" he yelped as she clamped her teeth onto his hand. And Vlad was helping, too, snatching guns from the soldiers too frightened to take him on.

So distracted by my supernatural friends, I almost overlooked the warlord slinking towards the doorway. "The Taotie, he's trying to get away!" I shouted. The others were too busy dealing with the soldiers to stop him. I raced over, blocking his path. I expected him to scoff and point his gun at me.

I must have had a fiercer look on my face than I realized, for his eyes went wide in terror.

Then I heard a *click-click-click-click* behind me. Up the stairs it came, a slow, steady sound. Then followed a deep, unearthly growl, and labored breathing. I knew what it was.

So did the one who stole its freedom, and its name.

"N-N-No, don't," pleaded the warlord as the taotie — the real one, that is — waddled through the doorway. "I didn't mean to keep you locked up all those years... I just couldn't find a good home for you! Except for keeping you in a cage, I've always treated you well, haven't I?"

The creature kept lumbering toward the warlord.

"I, I was going to let you out today, honest!"

Still the true taotie came, its huge sagging stomach dragging along the stone floor. Everyone just watched, frozen with awe — I could see fear even in Vlad's eyes.

"Help me!" the warlord begged. "I'll give you treasure, all the gold you can eat!" But no one would dare stand in the way of the long-imprisoned taotie. When it reached him, it opened its huge jaws and snapped down on the warlord's leg. "Aaargh! No, don't!" It began dragging the warlord back toward the doorway. The warlord's screams echoed quieter and quieter as he was dragged away down the stairs, until we heard no more.

From below came the sounds of a great battle. I dashed over to the edge and saw the orderly ranks of the warlord's army exploding into chaos. The creatures of the Garden, prisoners no longer, charged and flew at them, the qilin piercing the trucks and cannons with its antlers, the Russian household spirit scattering troops, the merman shaking his fists. Even the Firebird joined in, pulling along its trail of flames, swooping and dive-bombing the tanks driving off in a vain attempt to escape. The soldiers scattered every which way. As if by magic — which it was, I guess — the warlord's army was coming apart at the seams.

After destroying the planes, the Firebird, majestic and terrible, soared up, level with the battlements, and gave me one last look before it flew off into the pink dawn. Then it turned and, in a moment, there was only a red-gold brilliance lingering in the sky, until it, like the threat to Peking, faded to nothing.

29

The Reunion

"What a mess! Not much to my liking, but that should just about take care of things."

I turned to the woman who had spoken, now standing beside me. "Kang! Thank you!"

She gave me her dimpled smile, once again in her human guise. Or was human her natural form? I decided it didn't matter, all that did was that she had come when we needed her most.

Vlad shuffled over. "Our little brawl has taken just about the last out of me," he said. Wheezing and drooping, he leaned against a wall. "Though I declare it well worth it."

"But how did you get out of your cages?" I asked.

"That was me," said another voice.

Su! I ran over and hugged her as she stepped onto the battlements.

"It worked, you got out! Tell me what happened?"

"After I unlocked the chains, I was trying to think of some way I could help you. I decided, when you face a particularly difficult situation, sometimes you need a few more friends to help out." She held up the warlord's master key. "This worked on all the cages. You'd think he'd be more careful, but he was just too lazy and overconfident."

"Brilliant, Su!" Even as I said it, something was tugging at my elation. We had defeated the warlord, but where was my father?

Vlad seemed to read my mind. "Seek answers from him," he said, pointing to a soldier rubbing the back of his head as he came to. It was Piggy Eyes.

I went over, followed by Su, Vlad, and Kang. Seeing us all—well, seeing Vlad and Kang—Piggy Eyes tried to hide his terror, but with his trembling lips and shaking hands, did a poor job of it. "My father, where is he?" I demanded.

"If-if-if I tell you, th-th-that crazy f-fox won't come at me again?" That arrogant smile of his was nowhere to be seen now.

I put my arm around Kang. "I might be able to persuade her—if you start talking right now."

Piggy Eyes nodded eagerly and was assured enough to stop stammering. "At the bottom of the fortress, deep underground, there is a dungeon. He's in there." Piggy Eyes gave directions, including how to find a hidden hatch on the ground floor, which led below.

"All right, off with you," Vlad snapped at him and the other soldiers. "If you make more trouble, do not doubt for a moment that my friends and I will find you." The soldiers shot to their feet and practically flew down the stairs.

"I'll come with you, Lucy," Su volunteered, handing me the master key. "How about you two?" she asked Kang and Vlad.

"No. We'd better get down there and make sure our friends don't get too carried away," Kang replied.

"If you say so," Vlad added, a little disappointed. Kang giggled as they departed.

On the way down, I filled Su in on all that had happened. About being captured by the warlord, about the firebird and Luba coming to life.

"You were very brave, Lucy," Su said. "Clever and brave. I would have never escaped if you hadn't first."

"I just hope we are not too late for Papa."

We followed the soldier's directions and on the ground level found a heavy iron hatch set into the floor in just the place Piggy Eyes had said. Su and I heaved it open, releasing a whiff of stagnant air. I peeked in. A ladder descended into a dismal domain lit by torches. No matter, with a surge of glee I started climbing down the ladder. Su hovered at the opening, not moving.

"What's wrong?" I asked. "Aren't you coming?"

"This last part of the journey, you should make alone." Her voice carried a strange tone, a little bit distant or sad, perhaps. "I wouldn't belong there."

I paused on the ladder, and my excitement of a moment ago shook beneath waves of sadness. In an instant I understood that reuniting with Papa would fill me with joy, but it would also irrevocably change my future. We would leave China. We would find a home elsewhere. Su, my best friend, without whom I couldn't have even started this wild adventure, must stay behind. Why did everything have to be so complicated and bittersweet? I thought back to when I first received Papa's letter, how I had felt joy and apprehension all at once. Even wonderful things, I learned at that moment, can cost you dearly.

After our fight over Luba, when Su insisted on continuing with me to find Papa, she knew it would help bring about the end of our friendship. If we succeeded, everything would change. But she was only focused on being my friend and aiding me when I needed her most.

"Go on, Lucy," she said, her voice shaky. She handed me the warlord's master key. "Go get your father." Whirling, she strode off before I could say anything more.

I climbed down into the darkness. At the bottom of the ladder I tried to take in my surroundings but couldn't make out a thing. "Papa?" I called out. My voice echoed tauntingly back to me. So

I was in a cavernous place but I couldn't tell much more than that. Even after waiting a full minute for my eyes to adjust, I still couldn't see my hand in front of my face.

I groped inside my pocket for some source of light, as if one of Su's matches had somehow slipped in there. Nothing but the feather. "This is your last chance," I almost said as I pulled it out. In annoyance I was about to stuff the useless thing back into my pocket, when I made out the most subtle scarlet glow.

As I gripped the feather, light began to gather within it. Now I could see that the dungeon was a labyrinth of twisting shafts and tunnels far more complex than where the soldiers had chased me and captured Su. There was not a soul here, no prisoners or guards. I started down one tunnel, wondering what miserable souls had once been kept in the iron-barred cells. But I didn't make it thirty steps before I was squinting—was the feather losing its magic again? Afraid I might get lost down here, I doubled back in the direction I had come. With each stride the feather regained its light, until when I got back to the ladder, it was brilliantly luminous.

Mystified, I tried another tunnel, passing more cells empty and dark. "Papa? Papa?" Over and over I called out to him, my voice increasingly thin with despair. Had that soldier tricked me? Was my father somewhere else? Or was I too late? As I kept walking, the feather remained bright. "Oh!" I said aloud. "You're showing me the way." I continued on, winding around a bend and then facing a long line of cells ahead of me. Then, like a comet crashing into the sea, the feather suddenly extinguished itself.

"No!" With the dying of that light despair squeezed my heart. But, what was that, down at the last of the cells?

Some sort of flicker.

"Papa?" I called, my hope almost at an end.

"Belushka!"

"Papa!" I ran down to the last cell. When I reached it and looked through the bars, my breath came up short. He was chained to a chair, with his back facing me. A stubby candle burnt almost down to the wick fought a losing battle with the darkness.

"Lucy, is it really you? I heard you calling but I thought I was dreaming. But how can this be?"

"I'll tell you, Papa, but for now let's get you out of there! The warlord is defeated!"

My hands were shaking so much it took me three tries to insert the key into the lock. I turned it and slid the cell door open. I fit the warlord's key into the keyhole of his chains.

Freed at last, Papa wrapped me up in a gigantic hug, the best I'd ever have.

"My Belushka!" Despite appearing weak he swung me around as I clung to his neck. He was skinny, not the broad-shouldered man I remembered. A rough beard replaced his once clean-shaven face. In fact, he was barely recognizable, but underneath the layers of sweat, blood and dirt, his neck still smelled the same. It was the smell of comfort, love, family. How strange, that of all my senses and memories, it should be his scent that made the moment real.

"My Belushka, you rescued me, braver than an army!"

I had so much to tell him, about the last three years and even more, the last three days, but now that I could share as much as I wished, I found myself almost mute. I felt weak and spent from it all. I think he sensed this, for he said nothing as I took the candle and guided him to the ladder. We climbed up and held hands as we made our way outside the fortress. Some tanks and cannons and trucks were burning, others were crushed into useless wrecks.

"My goodness!" Papa exclaimed. "What happened here?"

Recalling the dramatic scene I'd watched from above, I could barely hide my grin. "I think some of the warlord's soldiers decided they'd had enough of him." I didn't mention that these would-be soldiers were creatures most people thought lived only in folklore.

A lone horse was tied up at a hitching post in the field. I saw a hunched figure shuffling toward it and, taking Papa by the hand, I hurried over toward them.

"Oh, my darling! How I've missed you!" Dusha gave off an excited whinny as Vlad stroked her ears. Now it was my turn to smile as Vlad wrapped his long lanky arms around the mare's neck and pressed his forehead against her silky mane. When he drew back, I blinked and blinked, but my eyes weren't fooling me. Vlad looked just the same as when I first saw him in the train station: tall, vigorous, and about the same age as my father. And I do believe Koschei the Deathless shed a tear of joy.

"I was in that dungeon so long, my eyes are playing tricks on me," Papa murmured. "A moment ago, I could have sworn that man was ninety years old if a day."

Vlad walked Dusha over to us and addressed my father. "From one former soldier of Russia to another, I greet you, sir." He extended his hand. "And I congratulate you."

"Congratulate me? Why? All I have done is gotten myself captured. No honor in that."

"Ah, but there is no greater honor than raising a daughter like Lucy."

My cheeks reddened like apples and I felt so overwhelmed, I had to walk away. As the two of them chattered away like old friends, I couldn't help giggling at how Papa would react when he learned he was actually befriending Koschei the Deathless from the tales he had once entertained me with. Vlad was no doubt pleased to find someone to speak Russian with who at least resembled him in age, even if in fact there was probably a few centuries, give or take, standing between them.

A fox ran out from behind a burning tank and scampered toward me. She tilted back on her hind legs, and so swiftly I couldn't quite make out the sequence of change, Kang was now hugging me, balanced on two slender legs.

"I see you found who you came for," she said.

"Yes, my father is safe now. But where's Su?" I asked. She pointed.

From out of the fortress, Su approached, carrying something in her hand. "You don't want to forget this, Lucy," she said, handing me what she carried.

Luba.

With a trembling hand, I took the doll. I thought back to how this doll and its secret cargo had sparked our big fight, and yet again I realized what a profound friendship I had with Su, and how lucky a person was to ever find someone like her. I threw myself at her, hugging her close.

Luba's face was immobile again, showing not a hint of her heroics from earlier. "You were right, Su, about the people who are gone watching over us."

Su seemed confused by that, but before she could ask anything more, Kang jumped in. "Your doll was helpful, wasn't she? Just like I told you back at my house!"

"She was! I sure hope I won't ever need her again, though. At least for anything like today."

Kang laughed, but a shadow crossed her face suddenly, and she frowned, as if she had just received a confusing message from somewhere not truly of our world. "Actually, I think you *will* need her again. Perhaps very soon."

I wanted to ask her more but she turned away. Wondering

what her comment meant, I returned Luba to my coat pocket.

"Now, my friends," Kang said, "I fear it is time for me to take my leave."

"What?!" Su looked like she'd been punched in the chin. "No! You can't!"

"Won't you stay with us as far as Peking?" I pleaded.

"Shapeshifters aren't made for city life, my dears, especially when they turn into foxes." She nodded towards the forest. "After being caged, I want to run free for a few weeks, living in my animal form, tasting the forest air, feeling the earth beneath my paws. This is my home."

"Will we see you again?"

Coyly she smiled her dimpled smile. "Now, that is a riddle I am sure you can solve." As she strode off towards the forest, she turned and waved, then disappeared amidst the green.

Su and I looked at each other. "Don't worry, Su. We'll meet her again. I'm sure of it." She nodded doubtfully. "Now come on, it's time you meet my father."

I took her over to Papa, who was still chatting with Vlad like they were old friends. Seeing us approach, Vlad mumbled something about finding more horses and walked away.

Papa smiled at Su as I told him, "This is Su. Ever since I found out you were in trouble, she has always been right by my side. She saved my life again and again, and I would have never made it here without her. I won't ever have a better friend." Just saying it brought tears to my eyes.

"Yes, I can tell, Lucy," Papa said. "Su is a friend for life." He turned to her, bowed deeply, and said, "*Hsieh hsieh*," thanking her in Chinese. The two could not directly communicate, yet the next moments were so full of feeling, words wouldn't have been much use anyhow.

Vlad appeared and cleared his throat. "There are other horses in stables at the rear. Unless you'd prefer a very long walk back to Peking."

We walked over to the stables, where we found a dozen horses. Vlad and my father saddled three up. I walked over to a short, cream-white horse and stroked its scruffy mane. I found a stool and managed to climb on and ride her out.

I gave a gentle touch of my heels. That was all she needed to trot off. It seemed that even the animals wanted to be done with this cursed place.

30

THE PARTING

"Is it me, or has that man gotten younger in the last ten minutes?"

We had been riding about an hour and Papa kept stealing glances at Vlad, until at last he leaned over and whispered that to me. "Something really is quite strange here," he added, shaking his head.

"If you think that's strange, Papa, wait until you hear the story I have for you!"

"Now it is you telling the tales, Lucy," he said, grinning proudly, "not the other way around. Just as it should be. I'm quite intrigued."

The horses clip-clopped along and soon the fortress was far behind us. I decided to tell him everything. Well, except for the things he'd need some time to believe, which, on reflection, included probably most of the events of our journey. I told him of crossing the bridge, being baffled by the riddles that had to be cracked to gain admission to the tree house and most of what happened in the fortress, except I didn't elaborate about just who—or what—was also being held prisoner. And as we guided our horses over the rolling hills, I asked Papa about what had happened to him on his train ride. He was silent for a while before he spoke.

"Most of the trip was unremarkable. About the only thing I remember was my wish that the train might sprout wings so I could simply fly to you faster, Belushka. But eventually we were getting pretty close to Peking. Another five hours on the train or so. I could barely sit still, such was my excitement at seeing you. In fact, I was so focused on that, I didn't notice what was about to happen." He frowned, a little upset with himself. "Suddenly the train screeched to a halt. Soldiers came pouring in from every direction, and in no time, they had seized the train. A thug with a rifle shoved the barrel in my face. Well, I can't say I much liked that, and I took the gun away from him and tossed him out of a window. I then got some of the other passengers to help me barricade the doors, until we were pretty well secure inside that train car." That sounded like the Papa I knew.

"But the soldiers threatened to hurt passengers from other cars if we didn't surrender, and I knew they meant it. I hated to give up but there was no way to go on without innocent bloodshed. I have seen my fair share of that already in the wars. Along with the other men, I was driven off the train, bound with ropes and taken away in a truck. When I saw the train continuing on to Peking without me, I thought my heart might stop beating.

"We were taken along a road beside a vast, dark forest until we came to the fortress. I was brought before that petty little warlord. Someone reported what I had done on the train and he told me I should be in his army and train and lead his men. Of course I refused, and that's when he put me in the cell and threatened your life." For a moment he went quiet, then continued in a strained voice. "I almost broke while I was held there. The thought of never seeing you again was the cruelest torture."

"I would never have known you were on that train, Papa, if you hadn't left the feather."

"Hmm? What feather?"

"The one from the train. You know, the Firebird feather."

He gave me a startled look. "How did you know I'd been thinking about the Firebird?"

"What do you mean?"

"Now that's *very* strange. While on the train, just before those soldiers attacked, I'd been remembering how I used to tell you stories before bed. And how the last night we were together, I was telling you about the Firebird, probably for the fiftieth time. In fact, at the very moment of the first gunshot from the soldiers, I'd been wondering whether or not you would like me to tell you the Firebird story, or whether you had outgrown it."

"I could never outgrow your stories, Papa. Anyhow," I glanced in Vlad's direction, "age, well, I suppose it moves in more than one direction."

"Apparently," Papa laughed, shaking his head. "But Belushka, I am glad that there is still room for fairytales in your heart. And that hardship didn't stomp out their spark."

Little did Papa know that their fire only glowed more brightly, flames etched in my mind after seeing the Firebird more clearly than ever my imagination could have pictured it.

As to the mystery of the feather, I had no idea what it meant, but I decided some things didn't need to be understood, only accepted.

Later that day, we came to a fork. To the left was the road we'd not traveled, alongside the forest. To the right, a dusty path leading into the dense expanse of trees. This time there was no need for haste, so we followed well behind Papa when he veered left without even deliberating on it. "Where is Vlad?"

Several moments went by before I realized Vlad was still stopped, as if paralyzed, at the fork. Su and I doubled back to him. Across his face stormed conflicting emotions.

"My friends, this is where I leave you. The forest is calling for my return."

"Why?" I protested. There was a pit in my stomach. It had been hard saying goodbye to Kang, but I found the idea of parting with Vlad dreadful. "You have your casino to run, don't you? You can't just leave everything behind! I thought you liked ... that you liked Peking."

"Oh, I do like Peking." He winked. "And yes, I've even grown to like a few people there, even if they cause a great deal of trouble."

"Then why?"

"Our adventure together has reminded me that Koschei is not of the city. The war is over and I can't hide from my destiny forever."

"What will happen to you? What if you can't go home like us?"

"I'll always have a home as long as people continue to tell my story. Promise you will do that? Write about me in books, tell your children my name. Maybe even mention that I wasn't all bad."

An unexpected tear trickled down my cheek. Never had I dreamed of crying over a sorcerer's departure. "Before you go," I managed to say, sniffing and blotting my tears, "there's one question I have always wanted to ask, but I haven't, because I don't want you to take it the wrong way."

His eyebrows arched. "Go on, Lucy. If you can confront a warlord and his army, surely you can find the courage to ask me a question."

"All right. Why did you help us? You are not exactly famous for your generosity."

His laughter melted some of the ice forming in my heart. "Oh, evil sorcerers suffer so unfairly — can't we be helpful every now and again without ruining our reputation? Besides, I've always had a weakness for Russian girls who trample over gambling tables, causing an infernal ruckus."

I smiled at the memory of my visit to his casino, only a few days ago but it felt like that time belonged to a whole other life.

"Which reminds me: Lucy, please take care of my beloved wolf. Perhaps it can aid you in your next journey."

I nodded, knowing it was his way of giving me the beautiful painting from his office.

"And, Su, remember, the poet Li Bai unlocks many things, not only our souls."

Su nodded slowly, then jerked away so no one could see her face. Apparently, she too felt more than expected at losing our friend, as she attempted to hide a sniffle.

Vlad cleared his throat again and again, as if some words were caught deep in there. Finally he took a deep breath and released them. "Many years ago, my soul was stolen from me. For centuries I searched… I never could find it. But I think I have now grown a new one. Farewell, my brave friends."

He clucked his tongue and gave a gentle kick to Dusha, and they followed the path to their home. I was hoping he would look back before they disappeared into the forest, just for one final goodbye, but he didn't. I like to think it was because our parting pained him as much as it did me.

31

THE CHOICE

"Now that they are gone, I think I'll wonder if I imagined it all," Su sighed a few hours later. Papa was still ahead of us, scouting. We rode slowly together, side by side.

"We know what we saw, and we'll remind each other," I said. What I left unsaid: for how long? Would Papa want to leave China for America right away?

"What's that?" Su said, breaking into my mournful thoughts. I looked towards where Su pointed—ahead, a giant hole made the road unpassable. I saw Papa riding back towards us from the hills to the side.

"Those are blast craters from cannon fire," he said. "I would guess that the warlord's men practiced shooting out here. We will have to go around. There's a trail winding around the hill. This way." We followed him off the road and onto a narrow trail which skirted a deep chasm as it curved around the hill. "It is quite dangerous ahead," he announced. "I've managed to move some rocks off the trail, but you will have to be very careful. I'll ride in the back, but you'll need to ride single file on this stretch."

"I'll go first!" Su volunteered. I knew she would.

Papa chuckled. "A warrior spirit, I see!" Reddening, though she couldn't understand him, Su returned his grin, still a little shy around Papa.

"Hey Lucy," she called. "Remember, don't look down." She

snickered and heeled her horse forward. We moved carefully along the trail, which barely clung to the edge of the chasm, yet I found myself enjoying the rhythmic sway of the horse. I was surprised how at ease I felt on the powerful steed. The surefooted hooves of my horse slowly rounded each curve. I let my mind drift, even momentarily enjoying the distant scenery anchored by the Great Wall of China. This was a striking, dramatic landscape, where millions of stories had taken place. Now mine had, too.

My serenity ended at the crash of tumbling rocks somewhere behind me. "Papa! Are you all right?"

"Yes, fine! There was a rockslide. I can't get through yet. Just hang on, I'll be there soon."

I was about to call to Su to let her know when –

"Help!"

It was Su.

"What's wrong?" I cried, urging my horse ahead. As I rounded the bend, I yanked on my reins, my jaw dropping.

"Not too close, Lucy," Su said in a quaking voice. Her feet were scrabbling at the precipice, trying to find solid ground, as a familiar figure gripped her by the throat. His belly was even bigger than before and his mole hair whipped like a flag in the wind. "I was wrong before," Su went on shakily. "He is not a grave-robber—he is a hungry ghost!"

"Hungry for what?" I cried, but Su was too busy trying to keep her footing to answer. "What do you want?" I demanded of him.

Turning toward me, he smiled a ghastly smile. "A pleasure to see you again. I wish it were under better circumstances, but you know I have my needs. Here you are, safe and sound—thanks to my help. Now, just as we agreed, I shall name my price." He extended his skinny arms, with Su's feet dangling in the empty air. She shook with fear, an unfamiliar look for my brave friend.

"After seeing it in my cave, I just couldn't stop thinking about it. It's nice. Awfully nice."

I knew exactly what he wanted. There was no question about what I had to do and though it wrenched at my soul, I didn't hesitate for a moment to grab Luba out of my pocket. His eyes ignited with a greedy fire. "Put Su down — then the doll is yours," I insisted. Yet I worried this horrible creature would not hold up his end of the bargain.

"Lucy!" I heard my father yell. "Where are you?" I ignored his cry, knowing I must deal with this myself. Arm shaking, I extended Luba toward him.

The ravenous eyes of the ghost lit up and he hurled Su back onto the path, and in the same motion snatched the doll from me. "Why, thank you so much!" he said laughingly. "Terribly kind of you." He held up Luba, staring at her face, but then his greedy grin faltered. Placing his nose on her, he took several big sniffs. "Mischief. She stinks of it. She'll be too much trouble." Roughly he tore open Luba's belly and scooped out the jewels hidden inside. Without another word he jumped off the ledge. I ran over and saw him easily land, despite dropping fifty feet, and then scurry away at an impossible speed.

I raced over to Su, her back against the rock wall, taking deep breaths to recover from her fright. "Lucy, I'm so sorry, I just didn't see him and I didn't have time to get away. I thought we were done with these types and let my guard down." She looked shattered by guilt. "You gave up all the jewels for me. I know what they meant for you and your father. You were going to start a new life."

"Well, a true friend is the greatest fortune you can have. You taught me that. Remember our oath?"

Su sniffled and nodded. And as if we shared one mind, without asking the other, we began reciting part of the oath together:

> *"I want to be your friend*
> *Forever and ever without break or decay*
> *When the hills are all flat*
> *And the rivers are all dry,*
> *When it lightnings and thunders in winter*
> *When it rains and snows in summer.*
> *When Heaven and Earth mingle*
> *Not till then will I part from you."*

Papa ran up just as we finished, startled to find us reciting Chinese poetry together. I explained what had happened in the broadest terms possible, deciding at the last moment to leave out the part of the hungry ghost, saying a bandit robbed us — I figured Papa had been through enough and could only take so much today.

I returned Luba to my pocket. I decided I would tell no one of her magic, of how she had saved us all. Not even Su. That secret would be sewn in me forever.

32

THE FUTURE

A couple days of easy, happily uneventful riding later, Peking rose in the distance. It looked to me to cast a new shadow today, with a brighter sun.

Entering the city on horseback, I felt the warm embrace of the familiar sights, aromas, and sounds. Papa was wide-eyed at the bustling streets around him. I'd forgotten this was a new world for him. We decided to go directly home as Su was anxious to be reunited with her father, whom she knew would be worried sick. Walking into the familiar courtyard with Papa by my side, my heart felt full. I watched as Su and her father embraced tightly, joyously together again.

As we crossed the courtyard, I saw Su take her father's hand, gently guiding him to the house. Following her lead, I grasped Papa's hand, leading him to our front door. Inside it was much how I remembered it. The brittle wooden chairs and wobbly table still in the same place, but there was a conspicuous absence. Only faint clues remained of Madam Korchigina's presence, like her huge soup pot and a scrap of sheet music on the floor dirtied with a shoeprint. Her trunk, clothes, mirror, hairbrush and books had all disappeared.

"Korchigina must have thought I wasn't coming back," I said, looking at Papa as he lit a match. "She jumped at the chance to escape from me before it was too late."

"Well, at least she left oil in the lamp for us," he joked as he inspected the small house.

"It's not a real home, like in St Petersburg," I said, ashamed, as if the ramshackle quarters were my doing.

He set down the lamp and wrapped his arm around my shoulder, speaking to me in a soft voice. "Belushka, a home is not made from a comfortable chair or velvet curtains, but the people within its walls."

We settled in for the night, Papa lying down on a cot in the living room. I went back to my old bedroom, only a thin layer of dust testifying to my absence, which felt like years rather than days.

Despite my exhaustion, I couldn't sleep.

Papa wasn't suffering that way, for I could hear his legendary snores, rivaling even Madam Korchigina's. Quietly I rose and slipped past him. Though Su's house was darkened, I placed the smooth stone on the windowsill just in case, hoping she might see the signal and meet me. But I didn't want to interrupt her reunion with her own father or her recovery from the trip, so I didn't tap on the window frame this time. I walked the quiet streets, the city softly slumbering, pleased to be back in territory I knew so well. I climbed the old poplar tree and leapt down onto the dirt floor of the temple.

"It's about time!" a voice thundered behind me.

"Su! You scared me to death!"

"I thought you'd gone to bed early like an old lady!" She gave me a cunning look. "Well, you aren't the only one curious about Vlad's parting words."

Once again, she knew my thoughts as clearly as if I carried them for display on a banner. Indeed, the nature of Vlad's farewell was part of what kept me awake, that and the full moon. "All this wolf and poetry business," I said. "Naturally, he had to make it cryptic as possible for us."

Su began pacing. "Yes, it's like 'shooting the literary tiger' all over again. I don't have the slightest idea where to begin."

"I think I do," I said, inspiration coming suddenly to me. Su stopped and raised an eyebrow. "But you are not going to like it."

She crossed her arms, giving a resigned sigh. "The Badlands."

"Sorry!"

Without warning, she broke out in laughter. She had to lean against a pillar to not fall over. I stared at her in complete befuddlement until she regained composure. "After being nearly killed a dozen times by either a warlord or a monster, do you honestly think I'm still frightened of the rough part of town?"

She was right, and for some reason, this made me laugh so hard that tears welled in my eyes then flowed down my cheeks like waterfalls. All my emotions were mixing like ingredients of a bizarre stew, I was half crying and half laughing but not sure which at any given moment. Finally I collected myself, feeling an immense release, as though I could finally breathe after holding so much inside for so long.

"Well, come on!" Su said. "We don't have all night!" She began scaling the wall, reaching for my hand.

———∿∿∿———

We ran through the glistening streets newly coated with frost, from the outer part of the city towards its dark heart, the Badlands. We turned down the street of Vlad's casino, now dark, no jazz music floating out, no gamblers hanging around outside.

"Where is everyone?" I wondered.

"Vlad must have closed it down. I wonder how we will get in."

"Who but the warlord would ever dare to steal from Vlad the

Deathless?" I replied, and I was right—the door was unlocked. Inside, it was spookily quiet. A pang struck me as I remembered how raucous and lawless it was last time I set foot here, and I smiled at the memory of running across the gambling tables and causing such an "infernal ruckus," as Vlad seemed to enjoy calling it. Su and I made our way up the staircase. Vlad's office door was closed. Slowly we turned the brass doorknob.

Luscious moonglow seeped through the window. An empty tea glass perched on Vlad's desk, a ghostly reminder of him. I looked at the painting of the wolf baring its fangs and found it as creepy as ever. "There it is. Can you help me get it down?"

Together Su and I lifted the painting. Then at the same moment, we noticed something had been set into the wall: a hidden safe. It looked so solid, a cannon probably couldn't disturb it. I pulled on the door—locked.

"I suppose Vlad meant for us to open this?" Su said.

"But this lock, how can we ever figure out the code?" It was like nothing I'd ever seen before, a brass tube about the width of my palm, broken into four segments along its length.

"Look, this is a character lock," said Su. She tapped the different segments. "These are dials. No numbers. Only with the right combination of four Chinese characters can you open it."

Each dial held eight possible characters to choose from, I now realized. "But there must be hundreds of combinations. How will we know what the characters are?"

For a few moments Su had that faraway look when she focused deeply on a problem. She gazed out the window, then smiled and muttered, to herself more to me, "Because he told me. I'll try the first character of each line." She turned the dial and began to recite:

"At the foot of my bed the moon is shining"
Click — she set the dial in position.
"Is that frost on the ground?"
Click.
"Lifting my head, I look on the moon,"
Click.
"Lowering my head, I think of home."

One final click — and the safe door sprang open. A miracle, I couldn't believe it! "Su, how did you know what poem to use?"

"That was the poet Li Bai's most famous work. It's about yearning for home."

Rather than clawing greedily into the safe, I let that thought sit with me for a moment. I considered the poet's words and could clearly see the moon shining through Vlad's window, the very same moon Li Bai had gazed upon as he wrote his lines more than a millennium ago. I thought about what Papa had said about home not being a place, but people. I realized now when I thought of home, it was no longer the grand apartment in St. Petersburg, or of some house in a strange city in America, but of this new land filled with the people who cared for me, like Su — and now Papa.

When I opened the safe, Su had to catch me, because I nearly fainted. The pile of gold, jewelry and gemstones sparkled blindingly. A fortune. Money that could not bring back lost friends, but maybe could help keep some together. "I told you to be patient, didn't I? See, it was a phoenix feather all along. Look what luck has befallen us!" I smiled at her, not arguing because I finally understood that like people, this magical winged bird can be many things at once.

Happily weighed down, Su and I walked out of the casino into the Peking night. The gentle pounding of the Drum Tower announced the hour. We hooked arms, the moon lighting our path as I turned to my friend.

"Let's go home."

Appendix A
Chinese Monsters and Mythological Animals

Chinese folklore is teeming with all sorts of magical animals, monsters, mythological figures and gods. Here is a little background information on those appearing in our story.

Dragon—The most famous of all the enchanted creatures from China. Like the chimera from Greek myth, it is composed of different parts of animals. It often has the body of a snake, but with legs, and can feature antlers, the eyes of a demon, the ears of a cow or ox, and so forth. They are the masters of the skies, seas, and other sources of water. The dragon symbolizes good fortune and power, and also represented the Chinese emperor and often, China itself.

Fox Spirit—Magical foxes have been part of Chinese folklore and mythology for thousands of years. With their amazing shapeshifting abilities, they typically make mischief but occasionally punish wrongdoers. In a wonderful collection of supernatural stories by Pu Songling (1640-1715 AD) called *Strange Tales From a Chinese Studio*, crafty foxes pull all kinds of tricks on unsuspecting people.

Hungry Ghost—Since ancient times, one of the most important Chinese traditions has been honoring one's ancestors. Hungry ghosts come in multiple forms but are often spirits of people who died in some tragic way or who are condemned to hunger because they are neglected by their descendants and not given offerings of food. Their hunger makes them unpredictable and, sometimes, vengeful.

Phoenix — The Chinese phoenix, or *fenghuang*, is unrelated to the phoenix of Western mythology, which rises from the ashes of destruction. Sometimes it is portrayed as a chimera, with elements of a variety of other birds and sometimes even a turtle's shell on its back. The phoenix represents goodness and grace, and it was thought to show itself just before a wise emperor would come into power.

Qilin — The qilin is a mythical beast made up of several parts of real animals: antlers from a deer, scales from a fish or dragon, the body of a tiger, the tail of an ox. Also like a Chinese dragon, when a qilin appears before you, usually good things are coming your way.

Taotie — As Su explained to Lucy and Vlad, the taotie appeared on bronze cauldrons as decorative designs. Typically these showed a bestial face with two eyes but no mouth (even though taotie means glutton, a creature with an endless appetite). They are extremely ancient, dating back 4,000 years or more. Their exact meaning to the ancient Chinese remains shrouded in mystery.

Appendix B
Slavic Monsters and Folklore Figures

Russian folklore mingles Christian and pagan beliefs. Its creatures and characters are often darker than their Chinese counterparts. Here is some background on some of those who appeared in *The Phoenix and the Firebird*.

Firebird — The Russian version of the phoenix, its appearance could spell danger or good fortune — or both. As Lucy understood, the discovery of a feather meant the start of an adventure. You can read about the firebird in fairy tales such as "Ivan Tsarevich", "The Gray Wolf and the Firebird" and "The Firebird and Vasilisa."

Kikimora — These female creatures typically inhabit one's house, sometimes protecting it, sometimes making mischief. Typically a kikimora will hide in some dark, out of the way place.

Koschei the Deathless — An all-but-immortal wizard who haunts Slavic folklore, stealing maidens and slaying heroes. We decided to explore his gentler side. Read about him in the fairy tale "The Death of Koschei the Deathless."

Nightingale — A notorious bandit who is part man, part bird. Though he lived on after his fight with Su, you can read about his final defeat in the folktale "Ilya Muromets and Nightingale the Robber."

Rusalka — It is said these water spirits were once girls and women who had died by drowning. In some stories they tempt men to lean over and savor their beauty, then yank them down into their watery graves.

THE PHOENIX AND THE FIREBIRD

Vasillisa's Doll — For Lucy's doll, we took inspiration from the fairytale "Vasilisa the Fair." In that story, the doll helps the hero Vasilisa out of difficult situations, just as she does for Lucy.

APPENDIX C
CHINA AT THE TIME OF OUR STORY

The Phoenix and the Firebird, of course, takes many liberties with the past. The city now known as Beijing was then called Beiping, for instance — not to mention there weren't actually any monsters haunting the woods!

While we played around with the facts, it is true China was in a state of turmoil at the time of our story. In 1911, the Qing Dynasty collapsed after its line of emperors had ruled for more than 250 years. This ended two thousand years of imperial rule in China and ushered in a new era of promise with the Republic of China. But challenges gathered like wolves and parts of the country fell into chaos. From this chaos emerged the warlords.

Sometimes bandits, sometimes former military officers, the warlords gathered private armies and terrorized people. One, Chang Tsungch'ang, known as the 'Dog Meat General', used former Russian soldiers in his army — one of the inspirations for our warlord The Taotie, and his abduction of Lucy's father. (The lucky monkey heads worn by The Taotie come from the Shanghai Green Gang mob boss, Big-Ears Tu, another infamous figure from that time. He always wore three heads stitched to his clothing.)

Appendix D
Russia at the Time of Our Story

In some ways, conditions in Russia were much the same as in China. Russia had been ruled by an emperor called the Czar (it comes from the same word Caesar, as in Julius Caesar). The last Russian Czar, Nicholas Romanov, took the throne in 1895. He was a weak, incompetent leader and the changing times proved too much for him. After many pressures and years of misguided rule, the Bolshevik Revolution in 1917 swept the Romanov family from power and replaced it with communism. This meant great upheaval for the Russian people.

These events, more than any other, led to the writing of this book.

NOTE FROM ONE OF THE AUTHORS
ALEXIS KOSSIAKOFF'S FAMILY HISTORY
IN RUSSIA AND CHINA

I love old things. When I was a child, I was fascinated by the large, square, heavy-lidded box kept in my father's study. It was filled with a collection of mysterious objects from my Russian family. There were all kinds of treasures: a beautiful glass candle holder, an army officer's epaulets (decoration worn on the shoulders), heavy coins, tarnished bullets, old postcards from 1920s China and, my favorite, photographs. It was here that I first met my grandfather's cousin, Lucy.

My grandfather, Alexander, was an only child, and I imagine that being around his age, she was more like his sister. Lucy had intense, haunting eyes made all the more mysterious by the fact that no one knows what happened to her. She disappeared from our family story when, instead of moving to the United States, her branch of the family returned to the Soviet Union. Over the years, I've often wondered what she was like and what became of her. As a result, she became the inspiration for Lucy in this book, a character who is an amalgam of what I imagined the real-life Lucy to be: brave, caring, adventurous and loyal.

My grandfather Alexander Ivanovich Kossiakoff in St. Petersburg.

The epaulets and bullets belonged

My grandfather, his grandmother Sofia, and his cousin Lucy Abramovna Markova in Harbin.

to my great-grandfather Ivan Kossiakoff who was a cavalry officer in the Russian Czar's army. Sensing that the end was near for the Czar and his government, Ivan arranged to get himself stationed far to the east, in Siberia. He then managed to get his wife and son, Alexander, on the second-to-last train out of Russia to China before the Bolsheviks took over the Russian railway system and stopped all outbound trains. Like Papa in our story, my great-grandfather Ivan stayed behind to fight.

My great-grandfather Ivan Timofeyevich Kossiakoff.

My great-grandfather Ivan with fellow soldiers, riding white-faced horse at front.

My great-grandfather in Siberia, standing at far left.

Alexander and Ludmila (my great-grandmother) settled in the city of Harbin, which became a safe haven for many refugees escaping from Russia. Along with his cousin Lucy, aunts, uncles, and grandmother, my grandfather, Alexander, created a new life while they waited for the war to end and for Ivan to return. In the meantime, Ivan sent letters to his son which served as inspiration for the letter in our prologue.

Letter with illustrations from my great-grandfather to my grandfather.

Once the war ended and Ivan returned, the family moved to the city of Hankow in central China, now part of the city of Wuhan. Though my grandfather did not share very much about his childhood in China, I do remember him telling me a few stories about life in Hankow. He described the constant fear of warlords, and whenever one of them outside the city started making trouble, he said, "The French were the first ones to roll out their cannons!"

After the war, the family became "stateless," meaning they had no passports, no embassy and no country to call their own. Like Lucy, they found a home in China, a place to create a new chapter in their lives from the ashes of war, until years later emigrating to America.

My grandfather's stories stayed with me. I later shared them with my husband Scott, a novelist and historian with a relationship to China stretching back to his university days. After Scott and I moved to China, I knew I had to use my grandfather's life story to tell a new story in my own way. This book is a tribute to my grandfather and to my own ten years living in China.

ABOUT THE AUTHORS

Alexis Kossiakoff and **Scott Forbes Crawford** lived for more than a decade in China. Trained as an anthropologist and now a teacher, Alexis' research into the history of her family, who escaped revolution and war in Russia to China, inspired the writing of *The Phoenix and the Firebird*. Scott is the author of the novel *Silk Road Centurion*, a history book, and many fantasy, adventure, and mystery short stories. When not conjuring imaginary worlds, Alexis and Scott enjoy hiking and traveling with their daughter. They live in Japan. Visit them at www. scottforbescrawford.com.

Printed in the USA
CPSIA information can be obtained
at www.ICGtesting.com
CBHW010246090824
12912CB00013B/206